MONSTERS

Also by Karen Brennan

Poetry
little dark
The Real Enough World
Here on Earth

Fiction
The Garden in Which I Walk
Wild Desire

Memoir
Being with Rachel

MONSTERS

Karen Brennan

Four Way Books
Tribeca

For Matthew Kerr

Please direct all inquiries to:
Editorial Office
Four Way Books
POB 535, Village Station
New York, NY 10014
www.fourwaybooks.com
Library of Congress Cataloging-in-Publication Data

Names: Brennan, Karen, [date] author.
Title: Monsters : stories / Karen Brennan.
Description: New York, NY : Four Way Books, [2016]
Identifiers: LCCN 2016007109 | ISBN 9781935536796 (softcover : acid-free paper)
Classification: LCC PS3552.R378 A6 2016 | DDC 813/.54--dc23
LC record available at http://lccn.loc.gov/2016007109

This book is manufactured in the United States of America and printed on acid-free paper.

Four Way Books is a not-for-profit literary press. We are grateful for the assistance
we receive from individual donors, public arts agencies, and private foundations.

This publication is made possible with public funds from the National Endowment for the Arts

and from the New York State Council on the Arts, a state agency.

[clmp]

We are a proud member of the Community of Literary Magazines and Presses.

Distributed by University Press of New England
One Court Street, Lebanon, NH 03766

Contents

Night, the sleeping animals—
it all gets carted away,
sooner or later.

—John Ashbery

SNOW DAY

Today, everything you can think of in the nature of a regular day is made of snow. Houses have little window shutters made of snow and trees made of snow stand proudly in front yards. There's a snow restaurant where flavored snow is served on round snow plates and the waiters, made of snow, have charcoal for eyes like snow men. We drive our snow car into a desert of snow, camels of snow leaping around snow dunes, snow cactus all bent over from the great weight of snow, thick snow snakes writhing and hissing between snow fissures. It is all so beautiful that we fall into each other's arms and, in a flurry of snow, believe ourselves dissolving—as if everything were forever joined, forever pure and whole. A snow bird trembles overhead and we recall now that it cannot last. Just one day is what they'd promised. One day in the great scheme of things.

SMOKERS

For a while in my life, I frequented the smoking area outside a hospital trauma unit. There among a crop of skinny dust-filled palms on a concrete patio rich with graffiti, we lit up—dying people hooked to IVs, catheters banging against their hips, a few in wheelchairs, hospital gowns obscenely agape, and others like me, nervously pacing, waiting for word.

There was a woman pushing an oxygen tank. She said she was homeless and couldn't afford a new tank which cost $20. She was hitting everyone up for cash and from me she bummed a Marlboro Light.

A few gang members with gunshot wounds, arms or legs or skulls bandaged heavily, looked resigned, waiting for their release dates. They wanted to be elsewhere, but they were used to it: incarceration and boredom. They were not inclined to violence at the time. This I made sure of. I used to talk to one who'd gotten himself shot in the ear. His name was Pepe. S'up, he got to saying to me. Not much, I'd say back.

There were flowers trying to bloom in concrete beds. Zinnias whose petals had fallen into a litter of old butts. It made a kind of pathetic sight. That and the milling around smokers and the MacDonald's fifteen feet away with its long lines. It was like a bus station whose buses were permanently delayed. One of those places between real places where there always seemed to be one cloud in the sky, directly over our heads, as if it were a stage set we milled around on.

I was sitting cross-legged in the grass when a man approached me. He was small and dark and gave the impression of being so wiry he'd be able to tie his body in knots if he wanted to. He wore a bandana around his head or around his neck, I forget which. He squatted down in the grass beside me and held out a quarter. It's ok, I said. I didn't mind giving away cigarettes; I felt guilty about smoking. He lit up and inhaled deeply, as if he were smoking a joint. It amused me to see him taking so much pleasure from it. Cheers, I said. I could tell you a few things about yourself, he said. Right, I said.

My daughter was in ICU in a coma from which she might never emerge. This is what the neurosurgeon told me that morning. She might never emerge, we honestly don't know. Even if she does emerge, the consequences will be severe. The MRI will tell us more. The neurosurgeon was about twenty-five, my daughter's age. She had long permed hair and she wore a floral print dress that made her look like a Mormon wife. Still, I had to take her seriously. After she told me, I went to my daughter's bedside and held her hand for a while. Her eyes were closed but she looked peaceful. She was hooked up to a million things: IVs, intercranial pressure monitors, ventilation tubes, pulse, respiration, etc. You could look up at a screen above her head and tell how she was doing if you knew what the numbers meant. I made it my business to know and so when the numbers rose too high I grabbed a nearby nurse.

There was one nurse who couldn't stand me. Quit watching the monitors, she commanded. DON'T PANIC! she'd shout. It was her habit to slam things around Dotty's cubical. She'd open a drawer and slam in new dressings, then she'd slam the drawer closed. She even suctioned out the trach in a cold fury—jamming the suctioning apparatus too far down the trach hole so that Dotty's body would thrash and bolt in the bed and her face would turn blue. I should have reported her, but I was too overwhelmed at the time.

Seriously, said the guy with the bandana, I have psychic powers. I'm in touch with the spirits. At this he waved his little arm toward the glassed-in area with the picnic tables where a few nurses were eating enchiladas.

Huh, I said. I didn't like to be rude. Also, especially under the circumstances, I liked to think that anything was possible.

You've got to have faith, said the guy. He closed his eyes and spun around a few times. When he opened them he raised his arm and pointed at my face. They call me Coyote, he said. I go in and out. I'll bet, I said, and I wondered what he was on, booze or drugs. I noticed he had a tattoo of a shooting star on his wrist and another of a lizard on his forearm. He wore three rings made out of twine on different fingers. His nails were filthy.

The Trickster, know what I mean? He put his face close to mine and whispered, *faith*. His breath smelled like chocolate and smoke.

I nodded. Every Indian likes to think they're the Trickster, I knew this from living in the Southwest. Still, I told him about Dotty. I had nothing else to contribute to the conversation. He listened carefully, nodding, scratching the side of his face every once in a while, doing a bit of nervous pirouetting on the grass. This last seemed out of his control, like hyperactivity or a disease like St. Vitus Dance.

I kept talking, explained about the accident, Dotty's coma, the uncertain prognosis. I told him how she was my only daughter and that I loved her very much and that I'd feel lost without her. We're best friends, I said and then I stopped talking.

It was twilight now and against the blurred sky the moon came up like a new dime, and the people pushing IVs and those others sprawled on the concrete benches biding their time turned into silhouettes. Only their cigarette tips glowed and the occasional wavy flare from a Bic lighter. The guy who called himself Coyote had fallen asleep in the grass. I was waiting for the results of Dotty's MRI and I didn't mind sitting next to a sleeping addict. It occurred to me to say a prayer, but I couldn't seem to formulate the right words.

When Dotty was a kid, about three or four, we used to hang out at diners. While I read magazines and books of poetry from the library, Dotty liked to collect things—the paper placemats with the presidents' portraits, the sugar packets, a few straws—and put them in her yellow knapsack. In my memory of those days, the sky was always drab, the bare tree branches scrawled against it like giant, listless spiders. Even a rent in the low cloud cover disclosed more of the same grey, grey giving way to grey, an infinity of monochrome above us, composing us and directing our fates. Dotty's yellow knapsack was the one spot of color I remember from that time. In fact, Dotty was the one spot of color in my whole life, period.

If I closed my eyes, I could see her face with the freckles, her blue eyes with their fringe of dark lashes. I could see her smile.

It was unbelievable to me that it all came down to this: an MRI, a matter of intercranial fluid and blood. Whether a glowing blip went up or down on a monitor. The swarm or retreat of antibodies or the few inches from the brain stem to the first spinal vertebra. *O body*, I wanted to yell out, *Let us not forget your certain treacheries.* This might have been my prayer.

Just then Pepe sauntered by and held out his Camel straight for a light. S'up, he said as usual. Nada, I said back. He wore a fresher, tidier dressing over his ear, but now his eye was bruised and swollen.

What's up with your eye? I said. Pepe shrugged. Ain't one thing it's the other. An angular blind man was scratching his way toward us with a silver cane. I hear you brother, he said as Pepe headed off in the direction of the MacDonald's line, I hear you loud and clear. His voice had an amazing quality, like a TV newscaster's voice or a preacher's, only more sonorous, as if he carried his own private echo chamber along with him wherever he went. It sent chills up my spine.

Who is that guy? I said. The man called Coyote had roused himself and was fumbling for a smoke from my pack of Marlboros. But what you have to understand is that this didn't bother me. I was in that state of mind, produced no doubt by shock and sorrow, where I saw myself as one of millions groping along a dark, unruly plain, waiting for deliverance. Whether Coyote helped himself to a smoke or to a $20 bill from my wallet made no difference to me. In truth, it made me feel a little less lonely.

That'd be Roberto Mendez, said Coyote. Navajo, he added.

Up close, there was something courtly about Roberto Mendez. It was more than the voice. He was an elderly, slightly frail-looking gent—maybe seventy or so—and other than a grey stubble on his jaw, he made an impeccable appearance: short-sleeved sport shirt, wrinkle free and patterned with a neat geometric design, tan slacks, cowboy boots that, though old, gave off a deep, well-tended gloss. He inclined his head toward Coyote and raised one hand in a greeting. My brother, he said. Then he slid the crook of his cane over one arm and fumbled in his pockets for a fistful of quarters. A favor, if you would be so kind.

Coyote was up in a flash. Hey Roberto, my man, he said,

scooping about three dollars in change from Roberto Mendez's outstretched hand. You wanna coke? 7UP? Diet Pepsi, if you would be so kind, said the blind man. And be sure to get something for yourself with the remainder. Right, I thought, with some irony. I had my doubts about this transaction.

Roberto Mendez went about settling himself next to me on the grass. This was a complex operation since he was a tall man with very long, unsteady legs. He used the cane to balance himself and lowered his torso gingerly, the toe of one cowboy boot digging a little rut into the ground. I considered offering a hand but midway thought the better of it. People like to do things for themselves.

Once down, he introduced himself. Roberto Mendez, he said in his beautiful voice. I told him my name and he inclined his head. Not an Indian, he said. That's right, I said. Portuguese? he said. No, I said. I'm not much of anything. Ah, he said. Myself, I'm an Indian. Navajo tribe. He launched into a sort of account.

One year ago, I was living in Omaha. Omaha, Nebraska. I was not living with my daughter who had gone on, the previous year, to Chicago. From Omaha I was sent to Grand Junction, Colorado. I travelled by plane. I stayed in Colorado for six months—*seis mesas*— here he paused and repeated the Spanish phrase—*seis mesas*, that would be, in Grand Junction, Colorado. I was sent to a doctor for the purpose of curing an infection in my foot. I was having trouble qualifying for social security and I did not, at the time, have Medicaid. I was then sent back to Omaha. That time I travelled by rail. It was winter and although I couldn't see the snow storms, I could hear them howling at the train windows. I could smell them too. A bad snow storm has an unforgettable smell, like boiled milk or a drawer full of nails.

The blind man seemed to be drifting off. He nodded his head and turned away from me. He appeared to be gazing into the distance with the whites of his eyes.

Every word of this is true, he finally continued. They sent me back to Omaha, Nebraska, and then they sent me here. This time I flew. The infection in my foot had cleared up. But I needed and still need a prescription for Lanoxol for my heart. Still no social security. Still no Medicaid. At present, I reside at the Gospel Rescue Mission. I am waiting for an apartment. I am waiting for social security and Medicaid. I need the heart medication in order to sleep at night. I have what is known as atrial arrhythmia, an irregular pounding of the heart.

At this point, Coyote showed up with a Diet Pepsi for Roberto. I took this surprising return as a good omen. If Coyote could come back with a Pepsi for Roberto Mendez, then Dotty could come back with good results on the MRI. That was the flavor of my thinking in those days. Coyote was drinking an Orange Crush and laughing a lot. What's up Old Man, same old troubles? Same old troubles, said Roberto cracking his can of Pepsi.

I checked my watch. In a half hour, they'd bring Dotty back from X-ray. I tried to visualize her in her coma, but I couldn't—her old face kept getting in the way: her great smile, her dancing blue eyes. The yellow knapsack with its zipper compartment where she stored the diner sugar packets she collected. Once, as we were leaving the diner, a waitress inserted her body between the two of us and the exit. Your kid stole the sugars, she told me. She unzipped that little compartment on Dotty's knapsack for proof. These cost money, she said, removing the handful that Dotty had stuffed in her pack. I could still see the stunned look on Dotty's face, as if we had fallen from a great height, down down. This was a memory that never failed to overcome me and I felt the tears welling up, making the darkness seem prismed and shot with light.

Now Coyote had taken Roberto Mendez's cane from the ground and was twirling it like a baton, only it was too big to twirl and kept slipping into the ground. He was still laughing. Life is cool, life is cool, he said. He grasped the cane at the crook and, feigning lameness, hobbled away. Where's my cane? said Roberto. Where did he go with my cane? He reached out and felt around in the air.

He'll be back, I said. Except for the yellow lights around the taxi stand and the neon from MacDonald's and the thin, hard moon, it was genuinely dark now. I watched Coyote dancing away with Roberto Mendez's cane until I couldn't see him anymore, until the shadows swallowed him up. Next to me, Roberto was pounding the ground with his hand. Come back! he cried. His beautiful voice trembled. Where did he go? he asked me.

Don't worry, I said. Those were the days when I believed that justice always prevailed—that people didn't take canes from blind men and that one's beloved daughter, contrary to the doctors' predictions, would emerge from her coma without serious consequences. In other words, I knew nothing.

THE FIRST

and, I think, only farm I ever visited was somewhere in Virginia. My sister and I went with our nurse, who was not a medical nurse, since we were not sick, but a governess, though we didn't use that term in those days in America.

She, Nursie, was a thin woman, on the gaunt side even, with salt and pepper hair that gave off a steel-like glint. One noticed her hair particularly since it thudded to her waist and was perennially gripped by a rubber band. Imagine thick dark eyebrows, a faint moustache and knobby red hands and you've got the picture.

The farmhouse was an enormous plantation-style home, all white with a wraparound front porch replete with wicker rocking chairs and cats. The people who lived there had been former employers of Nursie and they called her Miss Delgurcio. There was a mother and a father, the former tall and blond with a brusque, stately manner and the latter an almost invisible presence among us, so absorbed was he in the daily newspaper and his cigar, except for the occasions on which he emitted a disgusting series of hacking coughs.

These were the days before obsessive TV watching and I remember playing a game on the living room rug. I think the game must have been Clue because there was a silver-colored candlestick and a tiny bottle of poison with an X on it. I remember initially losing to my sister and the boy of the house, which humiliated me.

My sister: younger, prettier, unafraid of dogs. The boy of the house: dog lover, sandy-haired, freckled. I had fallen in love with him almost immediately, but it was my sister he favored. His dog, also favoring my sister, at one point decided to bite me.

I remember the pattern on the rug. Big faded pink flowers and a green vine threaded clumsily among the stems. I remember the dinner table with its heavy silver cutlery and the bedroom with its twin canopy beds. Those beds belonged to Mrs.____ and her sister, Nursie told us, and it was a special honor to sleep in them.

This was the first time I'd been bitten by a dog (though since then it has happened a multitude of times, countless times, and I have made peace with the fact that when dogs spot me their mouths begin to water and they become enraged).

The cow that required milking was brown and white, like a cow from a storybook. I had such a book at my own home, in my own room, wherever that was. That farm cow was called Deb and her udders dragged almost to the floor of the barn which was covered in tan hay. I stood outside the wooden door, one of those half doors with the top half opened to reveal Deb and her milkers: first the boy, Joe, then my sister, who boldly reached under the cow body and grabbed a fierce hold of one appendage after an-udder, ha ha. She, my sister, was wearing plaid Bermuda shorts and a white cotton blouse. At that moment, if asked to picture my home, wherever it was, I would picture a child's drawing of a tiny house on a vast dark background because that gives you the feel of it.

My real home was nothing like that, but my idea of home, at the time, was primitive and unformed, as if my mind could not quite reconcile the desolate notion of home along with its actual imprint on memory. The notion of home for me had always been difficult and lonely whereas my real home had been complex and bountiful with no smoke rising from the single chimney and no dark empty windows.

After the cow was milked we were each given a tin cup of warm milk which I did not care for. My sister's eyes were bright, the boy Joe looked down at her fondly. The dog who would eventually bite me was nuzzling her calf. Outside the sun was like a child's drawing of a sun, with rays shooting out in a circle. There was a fence and a field of cattle who were routinely slaughtered for the evening meal.

Steak, every night steak. Blood red and sizzling, then cold with the fat congealing in a thin film across the top. We were all given steak knives, very sharp with little teeth. Nursie cut our steak for us: tiny pieces as those you would feed to a kitten. I felt as though I were eating my kitten (the kitten I did not own and did not long for).

We had been playing Clue. I was conscious of my long, hideous face, my flat, dark hair, of the way my pajamas bunched up when I sat and the absurd, unfortunate design on those pajamas, which was of chickens and eggs. What could be more embarrassing?

Miss Scarlet in the library with the gun, I guessed and I was right. Joe shrugged unhappily but my sister, never a good sport, overturned the board, spraying the players and the cards and the weapons across the patterned rug. That is when the dog bit my arm right through the pajama sleeve.

After that, I was even less popular than before. The boy and my sister went off by themselves and even Nursie seemed to distance herself from me. I felt my life to be on a downward slide. I sat beneath the white canopy of my designated bed, feeling sorry for myself, tugging anxiously at the bandaid that covered the tooth marks of the dog and soaked up the blood it had drawn. In the closet I found a box full of dried corn-on-the-cobs marked Halloween and a box of photographs marked Vacations. I took two corns and a photo of a man pushing a wheelbarrow and a photo of a woman in an apron wearing glasses that made her look blind. I put these things in the zipper compartment of my suitcase, along with a white bottle and a box of silver thumbtacks.

By now everything has undone itself: it has been revised and reconfigured in that silly vat we call memory, in that ridiculous thimble we call history; it has been repressed then unearthed then made to look more tragic then made to appear happier, all yellow, as if it had never occurred except in morbid, self-pitying imagination. The dog, the boy, my sister, the nurse: all figures in a display I affix to the bulletin board in my study to remind me of my vanishing.

I have already lived many lives but this was one of the first.

DISTANT NURSE

On library card stock I have written either *Distant Noise* or *Distant Nurse*. The former, with its taint of oxymoron, suggests the story of an enchanted chainsaw marooned on a desert island. The latter evokes the severe hair and pointed chin of a person from my past.

THE RAT STORY

There was a story he liked to tell about a rat who wandered into a Japanese teriyaki fast food restaurant. This was no mouse, he'd say, This was—and here he'd pause to measure a length with his hands—as big as a newborn: a giant Norwegian rat. It was here in the story that she—since she'd heard it several times—would begin in her mind to confuse the image of a rat with the image of a baby. She imagined the rat, lying in a little wooden cradle, wrapped in a pink blanket, its eyelids fluttering, and breathing in a labored, dying way and at the same time she pictured a baby, dead like the rat, in a sad heap on the kitchen floor of a Japanese fast food restaurant. While her mind shuttled between attraction and repulsion, baby and rat, she studied his mouth forming the words of the story in a way that was simultaneously charming and off-putting. The rat headed for the kitchen, he reported, stumbling in a kind of stupor, and everyone in the restaurant got up and left. He, on the other hand, approached the counter to ask for a refund. Well, we don't know, said the girls who were in charge. These were very young girls, he said, very wide-eyed and vacant-looking. We don't know if we can give you a refund, they said. We'll have to check. Do you know rats carry bubonic plague? he asked them. We know, they said. Well, it ran into your kitchen, he said. We know, they said. But it died. At this, their dinner guests usually laughed. Even she laughed, but her laughter felt automatic and insincere.

THE SKELETON IN THE CLOSET

They were awoken by a noise that sounded as if someone were being strangled, a kind of squeezed gurgle. My god, she said. I think it's the air conditioner, he said. He was very tired, having not slept well for days. The AC was on the blink and the repairman was not coming until Tuesday. In the meantime, they suffered intermittently—according to the whim of the air conditioner.

He rolled over and placed a hand on her hip. His hands were warm and broad and generally she liked the feel of them on her skin, but at the moment, because hot, she was a bit repulsed. She moved away and wrapped the sheet around her, tucked the pillow under her cheek. Then the noise again: a brief strangulated cry. What the fuck, he said.

They lay in silence for a while, waiting for the noise to recur, but the noise when it came took them by surprise. They tried to listen carefully, but became distracted, each by their own thoughts. He was thinking of another woman, someone he knew and occasionally fantasized about. He imagined himself with her now, lying beside him, her elegant arms crossed over her small breasts.

She was thinking about her son, a heroin addict who'd recently written her a text message accusing her of demeaning him. Like all heroin addicts, he was a deluded person, she had not demeaned him, merely offered him help and encouragement, too much so, to the point of his taking advantage of her.

Despite the complications of their lives, they'd become lovers and now they lived in this house with a broken air conditioner and with many things that required fixing, repainting, tightening and so forth. Earlier in the day, they'd cleaned the shelves in the kitchen and tore off the shelf paper left by the previous tenants. She told him that no one uses shelf paper any more, a fact that seemed to astonish him. In general, she felt she was a person who updated him, but she was not sure she wanted to be that person. She liked, moreover, to imagine him carefully applying shelf paper to the shelves. She preferred to think of herself as someone who didn't meddle in the lives of others.

The noise again. This time a bit longer in duration, an anguished moan with a little glitch at the end, as if a person were choking on a rock. Should we investigate? she said. Yeah, he said after a pause in which he imagined the other woman had asked him to investigate, meaning investigate *her*. This woman was given to innuendo in all circumstances which is why she excited him. Also, she was long-limbed and beautiful and wore a simple white nightgown of a gauzy transparency which revealed her tiny nipples. I would love to investigate, he imagined himself saying to this woman.

There was a towel on the floor next to the bed. She'd dropped it there after her shower. Now she wrapped it around her body and stood for a moment in the grayish light of the room. In such light she could discern the expression on his face, his mouth set in a thin, downward-turning line, his gaze aimed at the ceiling: a million miles away. Are you coming? she asked him. It's nothing, I promise, he said, irritated. But he was rising nonetheless, walking naked to the door and grabbing his bathrobe from a hook. It's the AC. I could kill that guy. He was referring to the repairman who had said he'd fixed the air conditioner and then didn't fix it, who had said he'd come and then failed to show up.

About moving in together, they'd each had misgivings. It was this type of thing—his annoyed response to a frightening noise in the middle of the night—which confirmed her misgivings. As if she were imagining things. She did not feel safe with him. For his part, he was wary of her thin-skinned nature, so prone to irrational fears, so quick to take offense. He felt she was perpetually on the verge of breaking down, capable of flinging his prized sword collection into the yard in a fit of pique.

18

I need a flashlight, he said. He led the way into the living room which was inhabited at this hour by the same grayish light of the bedroom; it trickled through the slats of the wooden blinds like, she thought, a poisonous vapor. When the noise came again, each of them startled and put a hand to their mouths, as if choreographed. This time, the noise was more of a wail, sounding uncannily human.

It's a baby, she said, her voice full of wonder. Sounds like a cat to me, he said. Cat got caught in something, the AC motor, most likely. He laughed. But what if it *were* a baby, she said, would you laugh then? It isn't a baby, my laughter one way or the other is a moot point. In the dim light he perceived their empty wine glasses from the previous evening on the coffee table and he picked them up by their stems and padded to the kitchen. I still need a flashlight if I'm to investigate thoroughly, he said.

Even if it's a cat, she said. It would still be horrible. He was banging the doors in the kitchen, looking for a flashlight. God dammit all to hell, he said. In the car, she said.

Why she continued this relationship, she was unsure. He didn't seem to care about her. He spent a good chunk of his time on the computer, surfing the web. When she tried to communicate with him she felt his eyes glazing over. The other disturbing fact was that, since they moved in together, she seemed saddled with the attributes of the sensible, practical party. She knew, for example, that a flashlight was likely to be in the car. With ease, she located his glasses, fetched the coupons from the drawer. She was beginning to remind herself of a disapproving housewife, counting pennies, keeping track of necessities. He got to be the free spirit, which she resented.

He returned from the car with the flashlight on high beam and this he swept chaotically over the furnishings. It's fantastic, she said. What is? he said, but he knew what she meant and now he jiggled the beam over her towel-wrapped body. You should see yourself, he said. Do it in front of the mirror, she said, and they went to the full-length hall mirror to look. Little roving ovals of light jittered all over her, rapidly catching random parts—a hand, an eye, part of the bright green towel. It would be a good film, she said. Amazing, he agreed. We could set it to a text of some sort, she said. You could write it, he said. I'd love to write it, she said. It would begin: "They awoke to a strangulated cry." "In the middle of an ordinary night," he added. Atmospheric. Good, she said.

As if on cue, the noise erupted again; it had become higher pitched, wavering tonally and straining, with great effort it seemed to her, to articulate a few beseeching words. Wow! she said. Totally creepy, he said. Did you catch that? What? he said. Those words it was trying to say. Sounded like "oh no please" or like "go now" or "freeze" something like that. Don't be ridiculous, he said. His bathrobe had come open and she could not help but admire the nice package of his penis and testicles beneath his flat stomach. You need to cover up in case there's a person in there, she said. If there's not a person in there you have to give me a blow job, he said. Deal, she said. This used to be their private negotiation joke until she discovered he used the same joke routinely with other women—as a kind of sexy tease, she supposed. Still, she didn't mind giving him blow jobs.

The noise issued from the utility closet, as far as they could determine. This was indeed where the air conditioner was housed, among other things such as the furnace, cans of paint they'd not gotten rid of, a few boxes of books, a bicycle. When he opened the door, a wet, musty odor greeted them, as usual. Hello? he said, which made her chuckle and then made him chuckle. There was no light in the utility closet, which is why the flashlight had been required in the first place. And the roving oval of the flashlight beam with its modest halo did little to illuminate anything in the pitch black.

There's something over there, she said, referring to a bunched shape in the corner of the closet. Oh that's just the suitcase, he said, the big duffle bag. I stuffed it full of blankets. She regarded the shape; it was lumpy and irregular, not like blankets at all. Why? she said. Why what? he said. Why would you stuff the duffle full of blankets? He shrugged. Seemed like a good idea at the time.

She blinked a few times, a nervous habit she'd recently acquired. They'd vowed to always tell each other the truth, but he was a literalist and the truth for him meant not telling an outright lie. He felt it his right to have secrets. Why his proclivity for withholding things from her should occur to her at this moment, the moment when he told her about stuffing blankets into a duffle bag, she did not know. Certainly, blankets in a duffle bag were not something she needed to know. They did not constitute a secret.

On the other hand, this did not look like blankets in the duffle bag. She imagined blankets in a duffle bag would be smoother, less irregular.

Admittedly, she was sensitive to any implied secretiveness on the part of her lover since her son, the addict, had so often victimized her in this way. He never lied—he simply failed to say that he was using drugs under her roof, that he was shooting up in her bathroom, stealing money from her wallet. Once she'd found a needle on her kilim rug—it had kind of merged with the design and she almost didn't spot it. It was full of something—heroin she supposed. She threw it into the outside trash and then she vomited on the ground next to the trash bin, unable to hold back.

The noise, when it came again, sounded exhausted, barely a trace of its former self, as if worn out by its previous efforts. It was hard to pinpoint from where it issued, this collapsed sound, this melancholic exhalation of air that even more than a moan communicated its dire unhappiness. It seemed to surround them, him and her, on all sides. Shit, he said. I think it's the pump.

The AC is giving up the ghost? she said. That's about the size of it, he said.

She wanted to say, It's not my fault. But why would she want to say that?

Why would you stuff blankets in a duffle bag? she asked him. Hmm, he said. He appeared distracted, but perhaps deliberately so. It doesn't look like blankets, she said. What? he said. His voice was sharp, irritated. Why are you interrogating me? he asked.

He could not help but compare her to the other woman, the one he occasionally fantasized about. That woman was blessed with an incredible calm. She was more down-to-earth than this one. He imagined that being with the other woman would be what it would be like to have a mature relationship. This woman, on the other hand, was childish, paranoid.

Once more he shone the light into the utility room and waved it, ineffectively, over the room's contents. There were the paint cans, bicycle, furnace, the boxes of books, the bunched shape of the duffle bag. Then the noise which had at this point transformed itself into a sigh, almost inaudible, like the brush of a very light breeze, or an even smaller sound, like the brush of the tiniest movement of air imaginable, like the movement air makes when a person is weeping or even talking softly to him or herself.

I'm going to bed, he announced. He could not keep the testiness out of his voice. They were standing in front of the black rectangle of the closet door, the darkness creeping out to envelope them, as if to swallow them in its giant mouth. He shut the door.

The truth was that the longer she lived, the more hopeless everything felt. Her son the heroin addict, her boyfriend with his secrets, this house in its disrepair. She felt nothing would ever be mended, that no matter how hard she worked to remedy a problem, a new one would come along. In fact, the house was a metaphor for the rest of it—her son's addiction, her relationship.

I'm going to bed too, she said. She followed him into their room and let the towel fall to the ground alongside the bed. He climbed into bed after her and moved his head so that it rested against her shoulder. She reached for his hand.

It just doesn't look like blankets, she said under her breath. He sighed wearily. Go look for yourself.

The sheets felt cool against their skin. It must have been close to dawn because the doves started in, *coo roo, coo roo*, a sound they'd always loved. For the moment, she was not inclined to move.

THE VANISHING

He said he felt as though he were slipping away. Each day, more
slippage. For example, a little chunk of his foot may go, then a
fingertip, a follicle of hair, a few cells from the earlobe. At first, nothing
discernible to the naked eye, nothing the average person would
necessarily miss in the course of events. I did not miss these things,
these portions of him. He was still dear to me at that point. Eyelashes,
an elbow, the shiny cavity formed by breastbone and rib cage—these
went eventually. Likewise, hair. Then, on a blustery morning, the entire
torso and, after soup, both legs and a hand. How can you still love me?
he wailed. The wail was next to go, becoming vapor, then salt, which I
used (still use) sparingly.

HEADLESS

I was on my way to the bus stop when I saw the headless man. At
first I thought it was a trick of the eye: I was wearing big dark glasses,
possibly the head had been camouflaged by the dark trees behind the
man. Surely, he couldn't be headless. As I approached, however, I saw
that he was indeed headless. There was scar tissue on his stump of neck
and a little tube sticking out—for eating or breathing or both, I figured.
He was wearing an orange tee shirt and he was tending the university
grounds with a weed whacker. Geez, I thought. A headless man.

It was very hot that day. I was walking along without a water bottle and
it's likely that I missed the bus—I had no schedule—and would have
to wait. I distracted myself from these concerns by wondering about
the headless man. How had it happened? He was either born that way
(poor mother) or it was an accident. I shuddered to think of the accident
that might have befallen the headless man. How was it that he was able
to live without a head, without a brain, eyes, ears, nose, mouth? How
did he communicate? Possibly the headless man talks out of his ass—I
chuckled to myself at the idea of a deep, articulate rumble coming from
the headless man's ass. At any rate, he was gainfully employed. Without
a head, he was managing to do a nice job on the flower borders. His
body was well-toned, muscular, youngish; the orange tee shirt was well
worn but clean, likewise the sport shoes. I'd had a good look.

I waited for a long while at the bus stop, as predicted. I was really
parched. I imagined asking someone for a drink of water, but no one
was there. How would it be to ask a stranger for a drink of water? I
decided that if someone came with a water bottle I'd ask them to dribble
a little on my tongue. I'd really do that, I was that thirsty. I thought I
would faint.

Then two people did come, one was a young woman without a visible water bottle and the other was the headless man, who sat next to me, and who had a water bottle. What a dilemma! He squirted water on each of his arms, first one, then the other, and he rubbed the water into his tanned skin. I wanted to lick his arm. He also smacked some water on his neck stump. This headless man had water to burn.

Finally the 3 came and all of us got on. I took a seat beside the young woman who was a grad student in biology. All day she worked in the lab. No summers off for us, she said. Then she opened a book and our conversation stopped. The headless man settled himself near the driver in the space reserved for disabled people. Well, he was disabled, after all. He had no head and who knows how he did anything useful in life.

During this time I had a boyfriend called Mitchell. He was a nice enough guy but I couldn't seem to muster up any real passion for him. God knows I tried. We had been dating for ten years and we did the things couples do—dinners, movies, sex—but deep inside I was unmoved. It was as if my heart were a block of ice or a hill covered with thorns. From time to time I fretted about this situation with Mitchell, but mostly I ignored it. Who has the right to be blissfully happy? Certainly not me.

Now the headless man and I happened to exit at the same stop. Amazingly, he pulled the cord before I did. I followed him out. He walked across the street, which happened to be the way I was going, so I kept following. He was very resolute in his walk which I like in a man. I had forgotten all about my thirst. I tried to keep up with the headless man, but he took two steps for every one of mine, he was walking that fast. He raced to the curb to avoid a car whereas the same car almost hit me. I felt like a fool.

That night Mitchell and I had plans to see a movie but as usual we couldn't decide which one. In this, as in everything, we were on different pages. He enjoyed a rollicking comedy whereas I was partial to the art film. He liked sci fi stories about silly-looking creatures invading a human person's bathroom mid-shave, whereas I liked movies about confused people trying to find their ways out of the morose hands that had been dealt to them, the kind of movie in which everyone is doomed. Mitchell and I were built differently, on different premises. The premise Mitchell was built on involved a double-wide barge plowing through a roiling ocean, whereas my premise involved the shadows of trees that were about to be felled.

We went to a comedy because, as usual, Mitchell gets his way. If he doesn't he pouts. He has a very beautiful mouth and so the pout is not as annoying as you might think. Still, it's a bore to be with someone who pouts, beautiful mouth or no, so I gave in to the comedy which would surely irritate me. I am that way with comedies. Something about someone trying to make me laugh: I resist. Mid-movie, I go to the concessions and buy more Junior Mints. There I see the headless man. It was too much; he was walking away from the concession stand with his popcorn and I would have given anything to have been behind him on line.

The funny thing is that no one seemed to pay much attention to the headless man. You'd think they would. Headless! It was as if this movie-going crowd had seen headless men every day of their lives. It was as if the headless man was no more unusual than, say, a woman with long blond hair. He was making his way to Theater 8 and on impulse I decided to go into that theater too. I was bored with the comedy. Mitchell laughed very loudly and occasionally slapped my leg, god knows what was so funny. The movie had been about two men who were friends and who got into trouble. The trouble was supposed to make you laugh. One man kept hurting himself. When I left the theater for the Junior Mints, that man was all bandaged up which was also supposed to be funny. But here was the headless man headed into Theater 8 which featured just my kind of movie, one in which two women sit on a bed and talk for hours and in between talking they try on clothes.

I sat directly behind the headless man and so of course I had a good view of the film. I noticed the little tube that protruded from his scar-knotted neck had been replaced with a larger transparent funnel and into this funnel the man fed kernels of popcorn. Very strange. The film was not sad so much as enigmatic. Who were these women and why did they pass their time so fruitlessly? was the question the film posed.

I had quite a time locating Mitchell in the parking lot after the movie. He was angry I had left the comedy and told me that, as usual, I had been rude. I told him all about the headless man because I thought he would be interested. I told him about the jagged neck stump and the funnel and the weed whacking job. Once I began talking I couldn't stop. All my theories about the headless man poured forth. He must have a brain located somewhere since he is obviously functioning like a human. Perhaps he uses sign language. Maybe his brain was taken out of his body and frozen until they could transplant it some other place, like his thigh. He was really quite handsome otherwise, I said.

Stop, said Mitchell. You are talking nonstop so I will forget your bad manners. I don't care about this so-called headless man. You don't find it intriguing? I said. Mitchell opened the car door. Why would I? There are all kinds of freaks in this world, what's one more? *Unbelievable*, I thought as Mitchell started the car by doing this annoying thing he does which is to rev the engine very loudly three times. Then he backed out and hit a car that was driving by. Son of a bitch, yelled Mitchell, leaping out of the drivers door and shaking his fist. Honestly, Mitchell was such a stereotype.

I decided to remain in the car so as not to be humiliated by Mitchell's behavior. I turned on the radio and listened to the jazz station. Coltrane in the middle of playing My Favorite Things, which is very long, if you know the cut. Then Mitchell stopped yelling and Coltrane stopped playing. I decided to get out of the car and there, believe it or not, was the headless man. He was writing something on a pad of white paper and he jerked his neck toward me in a kind of friendly acknowledgment.

I swear to god, I think he remembered me from the afternoon bus stop. I smiled at his neck. Mitchell was still fuming, but he was fuming silently. The car was not so damaged—a broken taillight was all. The headless man resumed his writing, then put his hands together in a prayer-like gesture and bowed very respectfully to Mitchell. Mitchell scowled. There's not much you can do when a headless man bows respectfully to you.

The headless man had written his name, phone number, license number and the name and number of his insurance company. After all the writing he'd drawn a happy face. It was very neatly executed. He's obviously a gentleman, I said. What would you know about it? said Mitchell. I must say these comedies do nothing to put you in a good mood, I remarked, which was a mistake, because Mitchell drove very fast which he knows makes me nervous. I was clutching the piece of paper the headless man had written on and by the time we got home it was all crumpled and damp from my nerves.

At home, I got to thinking: the headless man had left a phone number, but what does he do if someone actually calls? I asked Mitchell who rolled his eyes, which I could have predicted, and cracked open a beer. Then he surfed the channels in order to find another rollicking comedy. What's the use? I said out loud, which was a mistake because Mitchell then said, What have I done now, what's my latest infraction? I went into the bedroom and tried to read a magazine. But in the back of my mind, I was still wondering what would happen if a person telephoned the headless man. In the middle of an article about why men stray, I wondered what would happen if *I* telephoned the headless man.

I took the piece of paper from the dresser top and smoothed it out. The man's name was Russ McCormack. Hello Russ, I imagined saying.

That night I dreamt about the headless man. In the dream he had a well-shaped, perfect head only it was made of stone, like the head of a famous statue by Michelangelo. Thus, he still couldn't talk or make eye

contact. He was weed whacking and I sat in the grass nearby looking at
the sky which was filled with more heads, all sizes and shapes, a great
variety of expressions on the faces—sad, angry, bored, sly, frightened,
you name it. Then I woke up. Mitchell had already showered and was
fixing his shirt collar in our mirror.

I spent most of the morning at my desk picking up the phone, dialing,
then hanging up. In between I tried to write a poem which began *the
headless man's head is in the clouds*, but my heart wasn't in it. It was so
quiet. We'd turned the AC off and there were no dogs barking outside,
no cars driving by, no mourning doves going *cu-roo, cu-roo*, nothing. I
dialed the headless man's number again, just to liven things up. The
phone rang twice, then there was a soft click. I said, Russ? *Russ are you
there?* I could hear the silence of his room at the other end of the phone,
hear it turning over and beginning again. I listened for a long time. That
silence went right to my soul. When I hung up, I could still hear it.

That night I ended it with Mitchell. I said what they tell you to say
which is: This isn't working for me. Mitchell looked stunned. He cracked
open a beer and shook his head. Women are such fickle cunts, he said.
He doesn't usually talk like this, but he was mad, I understood that. The
next day I left.

Funnily, I never encountered the headless man again. Once I thought I
saw him in the grocery store, perusing the veggies, but this man's head
really *was* camouflaged against the red cabbages he was leaning over. I
looked for him on the U grounds for a while, but then I thought, wait
a minute, am I really thinking of having a relationship with a headless
man? I don't think so. So I stopped looking and that was that.

ON LONGING

When I was a girl in ____, the year of the goat, it was raining. I wore my hair in a chignon; blue eye shadow; a sweater. I walked the streets like a person who'd forgotten their umbrella. The Ella Fitzgerald rendition of "Ship Without a Sail" captures my mood exactly and the streets of New York were mirrors of my soul.

I wanted to be an actress. I wore my hair in a chignon; blue eye shadow; a sweater. The sweater had a little row of rickrack, a crop of flowers with open mouths, leaves like steel spikes. It was raining in long lines. After a while I met a man who wanted to photograph me without my clothes on. This man wore a glowing green suit, a tie with broad stripes of gold and blue. He was short so he positioned himself below me, craning his head up to meet my eyes. I will pay money, he said. A hundred bucks. OK, I said.

The city, in those days, the days preceding the Event, was like a fairy tale. Little yellow taxis humped along like dirigibles. The man hailed one, flapping his magazine, then motioned me in.

I wanted to be an actress. I practiced saying "Petah Dahling" like Bette Davis and Portia's speech about the quality of mercy not being strained. On the stage I felt the noisy rustlings of history in my elbows: Sara Bernhardt, Isadora Duncan. Actually, I longed to be adored, worshiped and glorified, the same things God longed for.

The man's apartment was not glamorous. The laundry was all over the sofa and there was a smell; in the corner of the one room a cat had spun itself around a table leg and on the table itself were piles of magazines and soiled plates. I took off my clothes in the bathroom, then assumed a number of poses for the man. It was freezing in that apartment! The man took off his clothes as well—he worked better that way—and there we were both freezing cold with goose bumps all over our bodies. We looked like a couple of plucked chickens, as my father would have said.

I didn't have sex with the man that night since I was expected home, but I promised I'd call during the week. (I had no intention of keeping my promise since the man did not appeal to me at all.) I stuffed the hundred dollars in my bra and headed for the train.

At home my father was doing his various back exercises on the floor in his underwear. He was quite vain and when I walked in the door he leapt up and threw on his robe so as to hide his large stomach. Hello, dear, he said. Hello, Dad, I said, how was your day? Naya, he said, my day was very boring, dear, I went to the doctor and found out I have something called Cushing's Syndrome. It's when you have a big body and very small limbs. This made me laugh for some reason and as a witticism I suggested he liposuction out some of his torso and add it to his limbs but he said, No, dear, the doctor says I am too old for liposuction.

My father was 88 and had no health troubles at all, except those of his own invention. Also, he said, I have something wrong with my left eye, dear, because everything from that eye looks blue. Naya, right now you look blue on half of your body. But the doctor says he cannot help me with that, that I'll have to live with it. But it's very disconcerting, dear, to always see blue on the left half of everything.

I wanted to be an actress so I practiced with my father. I leaned on the window frame, lit a cigarette and exhaled a rigid stream of smoke. "Life is a bore, the world is my oyster no more," I sang. I fingered a Fabergé egg on the sill and made as if to toss it to the street. Naya, dear, please be careful, you know that is a Fabergé egg.

It was raining, as usual. The sidewalks were like sheets of glass that reflected not only my face in the window but countless faces in countless windows and countless cats and Fabergé eggs as well. The streets and sidewalks were like pages in books onto which the city engraved its little epigraphs or epithets.

For dessert the maid brought in choux pastries with fresh raspberries and butterscotch cream. I longed to play the maid in this role, dancing and juggling beautiful demitasse cups filled with espresso. I longed to play my father leaning back in his chair, his robe just opened at his chest revealing old silver ropes of hair. I longed to be worshiped, adored, and glorified, like God.

I called the man not for the purposes of sex but to retrieve my sunglasses which must have fallen from my pocket when I undressed. Oh yes, I have them, said the man. Could you come over and get them? Or shall I drop them off? I thought the former was a better idea. I didn't want my father to know I'd been posing in the nude for a pervert.

My father was a heavy man with tiny limbs who hardly ever got dressed anymore. He wore a robe and a pair of white boxers that were ironed daily by the maid. The maid was beautiful, full-breasted, swan-necked, epigrammatic. I longed to play her ironing my father's boxers or running the lamb's wool duster over the Royal Dalton. I longed to play her smashing a Fabergé egg, weeping, quitting.

My father shuffled around the house making what he called "preparations." He knew what was coming, of course, knew it was approaching, how could anyone avoid this knowledge in that day and age. Outside taxicabs humped along like dirigibles, and animals led people around on chains and leather straps. Flashing across the tops of buildings, if you chanced to look upward at the grimy rain-filled clouds, were parades of gigantic words in reds and oranges and neon greens. Sometimes only one word repeating itself like READY or STOP or HATRACK—their purpose to preside over the laconic lives of all of us who were repressing the future (as if to go there were to traverse the useless territory of dreams).

The man had cleaned his apartment, which was a surprise. The table had been cleared of magazines and dishes and the lump of laundry had been moved from the couch upon which the man sat. He patted the space beside him and gave me a smile, which did not appeal to me at all. Also I cannot abide men who want me to sit next to them on demand. Or anything else, for that matter including: blow jobs, haircuts, dinner. But this man had made a little meal of new potatoes stuffed with smoked salmon, which was very interesting to the cat who pounced on the table and gobbled up three or four faster than the man could shout RELIGION! which was the cat's name. Then the man became annoyed at the cat and took it out on me. I understand this. It's always better to interact with a human who will give you an argument you can smash like a Fabergé egg. What are you sulking about? he inquired in an oily, insinuating voice. I'm not sulking, I said, because I wasn't: My exact feeling was closer to incredulity. Surely the man doesn't think I will be his girlfriend, the man who wore horrible, radioactive-looking suits and served grandiose food to cats. Also he was much older, at least 60, so why would I date him?

You are not really very attractive in any case, said the man, so what the hell do I care what you do? Then I spied my sunglasses on a stack of books by the wall and I strode purposefully past the man and his cat who at this point meowed loudly, whose meow sounded like someone furiously ripping up a shirt. I suppose now you'll be going, said the man, contract-breaker. What are you talking about, I said. You got your smutty little photographs, you got your thrills. Some thrills, said the man. Shriveled titties like an old witch's, nasty little bush-bean, flat butt. Go fuck yourself, I told the man. Dirt-hole underarm, smelly mouth. The man went on, he was still talking when I slammed his front door. Likewise the cat: *rip rip rip*.

I longed to be an actress but in real life I was a typist. My fingers raced across the keys so expertly and precisely that at work they called me "Champ." How're you doing, Champ? my boss would say when I showed up for assignments. Here's a couple of hot ones for you, Champ, and she would hand me a few legal documents, someone suing someone or someone divorcing someone, the kinds of everyday interactions that both characterized and doomed humanity in those frantic days. Today it was a resume, very easy because the person had hardly any work experience or education, even though there was a very nice color Xerox of herself in a bikini affixed to the bottom of her letter of application.

In the background the radio was playing what we used to call "oldies," but which were actually fairly recent songs meant to create the illusion of a deep-rooted past. It was during the Bee Gees that the announcer came on and in a very formal and flat voice told us what to do immediately. Of course I worried about my father and could just imagine him saying "Naya, where did I put my glasses and what is that noise, dear?" because outside a clamor of sirens and other noises had begun.

After it was over, of course, we were all grateful. Even my father seemed to be lighter in spirits; he acquired a pair of silk pajamas and another Fabergé egg to celebrate his good mood. The maid did not quit, as she'd threatened, but instead let loose a flock of bilingual parakeets in my father's apartment, which were very good company. The man never returned my phone calls (I left my sweater with the rickrack there and to this day I imagine him putting it to unsavory use). My boss sold her company to me for a dollar so now I am the boss of others who are like the rest of us—longing for the rustlings of history to blast our lives with meaning.

SOULS IN TRANSIT, SOULS AT REST

She was pregnant and jokes nauseated her. When her husband, Guy, imitated Donald Duck, the bile rose in her throat. Likewise, she had aversions to a certain kind of TV show, the news in newspapers and conversation on the telephone, especially when she was called upon to initiate some action on behalf of the family. She had no interest in sex or in the sex of the child. Guy was a botanist currently involved in the re-breeding of the "broken tulip," a species whose varied coloring was caused by a virus borne along by a troop of microscopic aphids. She never bothered to learn the virus's complex Latinate name. She felt the learning of facts dispensed with the poetry. She wanted the tulip alive and dazzling, not measurements or comparisons to its sisters. She wasn't sure about having a baby.

Was she lucky or not? What plagued her was vague, non-situational, a certain cast in the sky or the sounds of the world growing haphazard. The mundane felt threatening: an overfilled coffee cup, a rumpled sheet, the flinty, fed up expression on the dog's face.

When she first encountered the ghost, she felt calmness fill her like a lake. At the banister, she watched a white face go by wearing a blue robe. Too typical, she thought. It went into a closet, she heard the latch click and considered following or letting it alone to pilfer the dresses and slacks. She'd been reading a book on breastfeeding, how to squeeze the nipple and palpate the breast like a wine skin, and therefore a bullfight sprang to mind, the only one she'd had the misfortune to attend where the bull was stuck with *banderillas*, then staggered and died on the spot. She'd been fooled into thinking the bull would not be killed, that it was feigning death. How stupid and gullible she'd been. Thus she went from breasts like wineskins to the bull's slow dying—first it stumbled on one leg, then its head nodded, then it crumpled like a tent when the stakes are suddenly removed. So eloquent, this acting of the bull, she'd stupidly thought. This was in Mexico. Now the ghost.

Minutes later, she tried to recall the ghost. Had it been a white gown? And the hair, what had the hair been like? She thought at first blond with a few tendrils, pre-Raphaelite, or a darker French twist, but had to admit she'd lost the hair. The face had been startling, but on reflection she was unable to describe it in any meaningful detail because what startled were not the features. Or even the pallor, though there'd been unmistakable pallor, blue-green like a plastic skeleton. What struck her was a jagged quality unassociated with the usual fear or anger or sorrow or despair, and so it seemed to her the ghost bore into the closet some alien emotion, but very powerful. It stunned her into calmness and caused a lake to rise within her, to slosh up behind her eyes so that she knocked against the cherry banister, holding on. Still, though, the ghost was typical, banal, its coloring like that of a plastic skeleton.

Guy returned in the evening with gifts, a new book on childhood diseases, candy, flowers from the experiment, not tulips but anemones with black eyes and flung in a bottle green vase she loved and set on the dining room table to pollinate her stacks of catalogues and white plates. She told him about the ghost and he loved her most this way, eyes shining, cheeks flushed, though about the ghost he was skeptical and patted her head which should have infuriated her but didn't. Maybe I did imagine it, she thought, because to imagine for her had never been an evil or shameful mistake, but something springing from a higher impulse to recreate and charge up the world. But she longed for the ghost to appear again because in another way she was curious.

Then in the wee hours, something blew the soaps off the top shelf where they'd not been handled in two years and in the morning she found them in the sink, one as if a bite had been taken out. It's the dog, said Guy, but how could the dog go that high and the teeth weren't the dog's teeth, she knew, but gave Guy a glass of juice and allowed him to pour and stir her coffee and butter her toast. She wore her dark blue Chinese robe with the fuchsia and green flowers embroidered on the back which always made her feel like Colette, and when he left for the day she enjoyed sitting in the window seat at the top landing of the stairs with a book and her cup of tea on a velvet cushion. The dog sprawled at her feet.

She heard the footsteps the next day—something running very fast over her head, which would be the attic. The dog was nearby and pricked its ears. Perhaps there were rats, you never knew, in this weather creatures tended to seek shelter, even a squirrel or perhaps a raccoon which she'd heard of once getting into a household and becoming one of the family. So she went to the attic still wearing her dark blue Colette robe because this was a day she'd decided not to do anything because she didn't have to, which she told herself frequently because wasn't the body at work making a baby and wasn't the job of the mother to stand by and wait? The attic was empty of all critters, real and imaginary and supernatural.

But since she was there, she pried open an old trunk that had belonged to the former owners and was stuffed with newspaper and read some of the pages which made her exceedingly sleepy—a forest fire, a dead politician, each story ran into the next. Even the dates blurred in her vision and when she tried to pay attention she found it especially hard to focus. There was a ruffle over by the small window, but it was only a thread of wind coming through to move against some fiberglass batting. After a while she found also in the trunk a pillow, yellowish with cabbage roses, leaves through which mice or rats had chewed, and a scrap of thin blanket with which she wrapped herself, assuming the fetal position, and slept for two hours that way.

What awakened her was the final fragment of her dream about the ghost and this time she felt shaken. The white face staring straight ahead as though it were either blind or saw something invisible to humans. She believed it had been gazing down the long line of its own past, its memory littered with stones and gardens and decaying vines, so brittle they seemed to crack the gutters from which they swung. She gathered her belongings then, for she had brought with her a number of talismans for the trip to the attic: the book on breastfeeding, the wilting anemones in their vase, a yellow sweater that last year she contemplated giving away to the thrift shop then thought the better since it was warm and seemed still to hold in its stitches some part of her life, a time in a Chevrolet, locked in a boy's arm, and then a meal which had been exquisite. She wanted nothing so much as to come back into herself unsmudged by the ghost's visitation, but it was not so simple.

The attic's little window was a sheet of typing paper and the trunk some florid passage from a book, sitting on a hooked rug from her grandmother's and gathering up a bunch of silver jacks, a tiny red ball. She remembered the passage which began: "And now, at dawn, I am casting myself into the presence of another." Still, as much as the mind was prone to wander she could not dismiss the fact that she no longer felt the same way about him. It was more than the jokes, the Donald Duck way of his to make her unsuccessfully laugh, it was something which seemed to shift in her soul, as in a tropism, seeking another direction. This is why the ghost offered possibility and a way of coming out the other side of a closed situation.

That having been pondered, she snapped the trunk shut and went downstairs to eat Saltines which were helpful with morning sickness, she'd read, and at the moment she thought she might feel queasy, a feeling that made the room seem off-kilter and diminished in size. Still, she was relieved that finally she was experiencing one of the normal symptoms of pregnancy (she could not help thinking of *Rosemary's Baby* when it came to peculiar pregnancies) and she headed for the pantry stopping once on the way to steady herself against the flowered upholstery of a chair back. In the act of pausing, however, in that beat when a person staggers somewhere, then grasps something, then experiences that first millisecond of relief, as if something in the body has been nudged aside in order to create an aperture to the light and, more importantly for her purposes perhaps, to *air*, she happened to gaze out of the window to her front porch, which was painted green and had columns, where she saw the ghost sitting calmly on a railing, raking her fingers through her hair which she now noticed and committed to memory was long and reddish and somewhat tangled. Simultaneously, the nausea evaporated.

Soon enough, he began with his cheering up program, once again imitating Disney characters and making a few to him humorous faces and generally annoying her beyond measure. She came very close to slapping him as he juggled a potato, a beet, and a zucchini whilst singing the Barry Manilow classic that begins "in the Copa, Copacabana." Instead she retired to her room, feigning exhaustion and asking not to be disturbed. The most terrible thing, she thought as she removed her watch and rings and dropped them into the silver cup on her dressing table, the most terrible thing, she thought, as she stripped to her bare feet and slid off her elastic-waisted jeans and unhooked her enormous brassiere, was when someone loved you immeasurably more than you loved them. It is this which stifles and chokes and fills the throat with bile. At this moment the door sighed and the dog's nose poked into the room and sniffed out the situation, whether or not she would be able to tolerate its presence, then entered and ambled slowly toward her, proffering its head for a few behind-the-ear scratches. The dog hardly ever annoyed her. It sat patiently while she brushed her teeth and dabbed assorted moisturizers on her face and finally, it climbed into bed with her and nestled into the arch of her back and began instantly to snore in a way that soothed her.

For his part, Guy sat at the kitchen table distracting himself with photographic plates of *tulipa*, reflecting that the variables in breeding were somehow equivalent to outside forces such as virus, aphid attack and so forth, deducing that in this way an equation could be made which might predict the characteristics of their future child more precisely. He felt despised. Her arrows cut him to the core. He believed himself to be enveloped in a feminine mystery whose arms tangled darkly around him and which he resented. As a scientist he knew he ought to be able to find his way into the light, which he yearned for, remembering a time in which the two of them poured over the pictures of Italy, the basilicas, the Madonnas, the yellow sky beneath which they held hands walking up big hills strewn with ancient rocks. Absently he doodled petals, sepals, and resisted thinking of her who resisted his best most valiant efforts to please, who resisted his arguably strongest and most caring self. He imagined going into the room and nudging the dog off the bed, but did not do this.

There was a racket at 3 a.m., which turned out to be the ghost emerging from her closet and scattering wire hangers on the floor in front of her dressing table. The dog leapt from the bed, exited the room, she heard the clicking of its toenails on the stairs, then for hours she heard it walk around the house wailing. Meanwhile, the ghost studied itself in the dressing table mirror and now wound something about its head, some scarf with a poppy pattern, she hadn't worn it for years. The overwhelming feeling was not fear but acceptance. It did not occur to her to banish it or even to question if she had the power or the right to order it around, but soon it left of its own accord and in its trail she heard a bizarre hissing, as of snakes. Then she was overcome with a desire to converse with it, to discover its history, its connection with the house, but it was too late. Oh come back, she thought in her mind, not saying it aloud for fear it would summon the husband and preferring solitude.

Guy slept on the sofa, essentially a kind man with a vision which included the birth of new varieties of life, because the amazement was in making this kind of thing out of your own ideas rather than watching them unfold as in a film. This is why, sleeping deeply on the sofa, wrapped in a camel's hair coat, head on the hard end-cushion which cramped his neck viciously, there was a feeling of it all being worthwhile, that is to say, the sacrifice he made or was making was like money in the bank. This kind of tit-for-tat thinking was foreign to her who dreamt instead of the ghost's white face, its eyebrows very thin and brown and arched wryly over its eyes. In her dream, the ghost was trying to tell her something. It sat at the foot of the bed and spoke for hours, revealing its story whose flavor was melancholy and even suspiciously melodramatic, she thought in the dream, but there were so many facets and facts they seemed to float around her head and then leave via the opened window just before she woke up. She had not remembered leaving the window opened. The dog had not returned.

Two weeks went by in which Guy refrained from the Donald Duck imitations and other attempts at humor and she was able to occupy the same bed with him snoring, along with the dog, two-toned throughout the night, with no ghostly interruption. Ravenously she read about childbirth and rearing and childhood diseases and child psychology and psychosis and educational problems and obsessions and paranoias and toys, outfits, types of sandboxes, and eating disorders. At the end of every day collapsing in front of her dressing table mirror on the small tufted revolving stool she'd purchased at the thrift store, she'd explore the changes in her complexion which she feared was not only darkening but inexplicably turning bluish.

One night she rose at 3 a.m. (always at 3 a.m.) according to her digital clock and wandered restlessly to the window where the snow was falling dizzily, and she watched everything below the window being erased by the snow. For a moment she reached out to the sill in terror that this could be so, that a seemingly benign force of nature had the power to obliterate while, at the same time, staying dizzily in the sky, within the line of her vision, and that there was no escaping it except to close the eyes. It was then that she felt a long, cold exhalation on her shoulder and smelled the ice breath of the ghost.

Suddenly she knew the ghost's name was Helen, though how she knew she could not say. It came to her with a certainty: Helen. Its name was Helen. She reached behind her to touch the robe of the ghost, imagining the texture of it like plastic wrap or even snow, but it was nothing, just air, neither hot nor cold. It came to her then that it had been imagined, all of it—the ghost, the cold breath, the white face floating through the room, 'Helen'—and that the fantasy was linked to the bearing of her first child. It was a kind of hysteria, she reasoned, that bespoke her anxieties about giving birth as well as the death of her old self, free of motherhood and wifehood, wandering aimlessly along the sidewalks in New York City where she'd lived for a brief ecstatic year a while back. She began to think it was a projection, the ghost literally the film of the subconscious flung from the mind onto the world of her house. The result: the ghost. Now the ghost had a name, Helen, and this name more than anything returned her to her senses and she saw herself as if for the first time, flawed from the inside, prone to visions and escape hatches.

Guy's head on the pillow had about it a solidity, a confidence that now attracted her. She saw in the curve of his lip that which did not yearn beyond itself and was therefore contented and able to give. For some time she stood at the window: on one side the snow's adamant falling, its white possession of the landscape, and on the other Guy snoring softly into his fist.

She was growing large and "noticeable," as they say. She wore Guy's shirts and some old green felt slippers she'd found in the attic. Now she thought more of the life inside, its kicks and disturbances. If she'd been a different kind of woman she'd have been comforted by this miracle, but as it was it terrified her, the savage nature of another creature growing beneath her heart, dreaming its own dreams. It was like the movie where things popped from pods and people died screaming as their bodies transmogrified.

In the attic, she stumbled on an old book on alchemy and studied for hours the arcane formulas for turning lead into gold and some absurd unreadable notations made by Nostradamus and decipherable to no one. The long beard of Nostradamus, his hollowed-out eyes, the etching which showed him holding an elongated substance up to the light all irritated her, and she wondered how mankind could have been so stupid as to fall again and again for this kind of charlatanism. Still, she studied the readings even as she disputed their credibility, predictions of disasters, the moon and sun changing places, all of it was in the nature of some badly written fairy tale.

From the books she'd acquired if not a *truth* per se, an *atmosphere*, as if she at will could be transported to a time past herself, a damp cellar room and then a landscape of fantastic wild beauty, of brambles and berries and a thousand shades of green against the sky which was closer and more protective. For this she was grateful. Since the ghost had evaporated she breathed more easily even though, truth be told, in some far-off corner of herself she was disappointed and there was an absence keenly felt as she opened the closet and rummaged around her former dresses.

Guy was involved in his work, which is to say a hardy breed of tulip having been successfully produced and symbolic of his own production, the child within the wife within the house, it all seemed of a piece to him. As for the tulip, half its petals were shaggy and the others smooth and the colors—purple, orange and yellow—she did not think beautiful, seeming to have an overlay of dust which made them grayish. Terribly proud of this abomination, the fact of his pride brought back her nausea, even though late in the pregnancy, and seemed to her inextricable from his monstrous humor and imitations and clumsy attempt to make her feel better. A scientist, he was used to accommodating the experiment after which he drained the implements and recycled them coldy, she thought.

In the middle of their dining table sat a squat bunch of these creatures bobbing their lopsided heads and having about them a disagreeable flatness despite the complexity of their design.

After Nostradamus, she'd discovered Madam Blavatksy who was more appealing and whose world, filled with astrolabes and playing cards and ivory lorgnettes in velvet and damask cluttered rooms, narrow windows reverberating with amber and green, swallows perched on the spindles of chairs, glass-beaded curtains and the surfaces of polished cherry

44

enchanted her. Dreaming one day, she heard raps emanating from the ceiling, thus in a circuitous process was brought back to the ghost whose reappearance coincided with certain fantasies: an unexplained warm spot on the tufted dressing table stool, a smudge in the mirror, as if the silvering had been obliterated or made to lose its reflective qualities, three white stones left near the doorjamb of the bedroom, forming a pathway leading to the closet in which dresses had been rearranged and/or tossed from their hangers and heaped indecorously on the floor.

Because she was not afraid, she told Guy that she was. He too noticed the dog's ears prick at certain times of evening or the rustle of something too close to be leaves. The ugly tulip had been abandoned and the present goal was more of the same with the aesthetic now a consideration. This for her represented a compromise, a sensitivity she had not thought him capable of and so when she described the ghost it was as if giving a gift long withheld. But she was not afraid and this was her protection from him.

From somewhere in the house, a music box began suddenly to play *Eine kleine Nachtmusik* and woke them. It reverberated in the dead of night, the tinkly precocious notes of Mozart, as if it were Mozart himself up and down the stairs in and out of closets. When they found the music box after looking for ten minutes or so—a time in which Guy was terrified and she was choking with laughter at his terror—she flipped the lid shut, and the music stopped then started up again then stopped. The box was in the baby's room, up until then uninhabited, and had been situated near the bassinette on a tall table for the powder and cream. It was a merry-go-round, a parade of horses revolving to the music, and in the center a long pole with a wooden flag also revolved. She'd found it in the thrift store along with the crocheted green and yellow baby blanket and the three old prints of grotesque red-faced babies in white frames which she'd hung over the crib. This music box had a chip out of it, near the red horse's foot, a little wedge the size of an aspirin, if that, and it must have been an old chip because the wood underneath had darkened.

That was really creepy, said Guy. He was examining the room for scientific explanations and finding none opened the window and looked out. She had decorated the baby's room in shades of mustard and green, a troop of camels and sphinxes high up on the wall, in a kind of border. The crib was maple and inside was arranged what Guy thought of as a strange assortment—a green enameled hairbrush and mirror set, a stuffed dog she'd owned as a child, its ears chewed down to nubs, a floppy lace hat, a box of crayons and three Oz books opened purposefully to certain illustrations. You'd better clear that crib before the kid comes, he'd said more than once and now he repeated it with his back to her, staring out the window as the cold air wafted into the room, and she wrapped her shoulders in the tiny green and yellow crocheted blanket just as the music box began to play again, this time with the lid down. Oh it's the mechanism, said Guy, relieved, and he picked it up and shook it but Mozart persisted in the wintry air, in the dark, for she'd flipped the light and said, Forget it, let's go to bed. Then they walked the hallway with the music box and the music and at the kitchen Guy veered off and wrapped the thing in a dishtowel and shut it up in the freezer.

Everything is a metaphor for everything else, she thought as she pulled back the covers, but this idea made her nervous, as if the world were doomed to repeat itself and she in it, doomed to walk back and forth across the same territory, both interior and exterior in different guises. That night the quality of the ghost changed, although she couldn't describe precisely what she meant by her sense of this. The air moved in wedges rather than in spirals. And there was rapping instead of apparitions. It was as if someone were hammering into the roof and Guy went to check.

Under the covers she giggled, thinking now of the famous Fox sisters who in the 1840s heard "raps" and "rapped" back to the spirits, by calling to them as if they were the devil: *Here Mr. Splitfoot, do as I do.* Also to have Guy checking first the roof and then the cellar to see if there were rats made her laugh. But the raps kept up, first a *rap rap*, then a *rap rap rap* and she believed the Fox sisters rapped to the spirits

46

by rapping out letters, one to twenty-six, a laborious process which she was not inclined toward, but which struck her as humorous. She began to feel sorry for Guy though not overmuch.

Soon the baby was kicking in time to the raps and this she disliked. She recalled that night looking at the snow falling and the feeling of terror she had, the natural world falling on the natural landscape, unstoppably, eternally. When Guy came to bed he looked defeated around his mouth, he frowned slightly, distracted, the look he gets when an experiment goes awry. But instead of speaking about the raps, he said to her: You never liked that hybrid, you made that quite plain. It was hideous, she said, though I suppose in a way amazing. But no, I didn't like it. I didn't think it was hideous, he said. It was 3 am and they'd been up all night chasing ghosts, but to him it was only a symptom of something else, her dissatisfaction with his work, her withholding of approval. What difference does it make what I think? she finally said. It's 3 am, what was that rapping anyway? It was a ghost, he said closing his eyes. Of course.

The ghost manifested itself in twenty minutes, sitting at the dressing table, she caught its cool reflection in the mirror, like a moon shining in the room, a nimbus around its edge. She felt she was greeting an old friend, she caught its mood which was melancholy and a little distant, as if there were nothing for it to do but to humbly reveal itself, as is. She understood it perfectly though if you'd have asked her to precisely articulate what it was she understood she would have gazed at her hands, shook her head. She understood the enigma of the ghost because she identified with it, she felt its feelings welling up inside of her, its pain at being disturbed late at night, its unnatural chill, its displacement into the world from which it felt unable to escape. She understood in the way of *being* more than in the way of *knowing* which would have required explanation. She did not, therefore, know the ghost, but in another sense, she was the ghost. Does that make sense? she asked Guy who was sound asleep and didn't hear.

47

All this thinking about the ghost produced disturbing thoughts of the baby. She stroked her belly with a forefinger, drew circles and hearts and arrows on it, tried to summon up that feeling for it, the feeling she was supposed to feel, because she'd read about it, the mystical connection feeling or the I-know-who-you-are feeling, but whatever these feelings were they were not hers. She could summon up nothing but the fear which springs from the feeling of being possessed by something that sucked and grabbed at her insides and would have happily choked her if it needed to, to survive. This was it—she felt, if she felt anything, its awful tenacity, the overwhelming power of its will to live. Did no one ever feel this before? Was she a monster?

The ghost was brushing its hair with the enameled brush it must have taken from the baby's crib. She noticed this absently, almost incidentally, for she was thinking of the baby, its brutality, pounding the wall of her uterus, thumping thumping. If only someone could tell her something about the world. If only this ghost knew something of value to tell her. What do you think about? she said out loud to the ghost and in the mirror she thought she saw the ghost smiling faintly, wryly amused. But Guy woke up then too and put his arm around her. I think about you, he said. Always you. His slab of leg went over hers and his cheek scraped her bare shoulder. Infuriated, she glanced at the ghost who'd vanished.

At breakfast, he offered her fresh blackberries in heavy cream, as if she were a kitten he had to cajole and tame. Her affection, lost to him, lost to him, he could not help gazing out the window at the aspen leaves rustling near the porch where also he saw the faint shadow of a woman pushing a stroller, or so he imagined. You had a right to hate the hybrid. Keep in mind that I'm a frustrated scientist. He smiled at her and resisted making a funny, self-deprecating face which he knew would annoy. Please forgive, he added.

Guy's work, in fact, had not been going well. In vain he tried to reproduce a broken hybrid with glorious natural-looking colors. Instead what occurred were wiry, stumped, mistaken shapes with colors that seemed oddly manufactured thus grotesque. He did not dare bring them home. Always more superstitious than his wife, he felt they were a terrible omen. They reflected on his inability to breed, to understand the process of life and death. Now the ghost or what simulated a ghost in his own house. Rats. Raccoons. Some wind coming in at an angle through some floorboard, coupled with broken music boxes and his wife's bad temper.

Was it a question of forgiveness? she wondered, gazing now at the same shadow of the same woman pushing a stroller. Whether he succeeded or failed, what was it to her, and she felt the hardness at the core of her being, her deep indifference to his existence. Yet his face was the same face she had once loved so passionately: eyes the color of twilight, as if a star could creep into them. His muscular arms, his throat so vulnerable in sleep, like a fluttering bird, she would often kiss it so as to protect. No, she no longer felt the same. All these aspects and more had now the power to dismay and revolt as if she saw from a different lens a parody of the original which to her he had become. Instead of replying she whisked the dishes into the sink and ran the water. Then she waited two, three minutes like an eternity before the door slammed shut and she breathed enormous relief into the room, going at once to the freezer where she removed the music box, cold but operable, playing Mozart.

The air was crisp as a leaf because October, season of birth, had arrived and she stood between columns on her front porch gazing at the mottled sky. The bright sound of Mozart, the leaves' golden rustle beneath, seemed not like a ghost but a portent foretelling her happiness. Just as, under certain circumstances, the world might incline itself toward a person, she caught for the first time a glimmer of motherhood—a certain exquisite texture and smell to match, a shape fitted into the curve of her body, a kind of impossible, glorious union.

It was this idea she clung to throughout the morning and part of the afternoon, going around in a soft bliss, eschewing the attic's gloom and the patter of the ghost on the stairs. Then she stuffed three maternity dresses, one pair of elastic-waisted jeans, a nightgown, two mysteries, face cream and toiletries into a backpack and left the house. It was her idea to check into a hotel, order room service for a few weeks, stare out of a window not her own, read trashy novels, and have the baby (it was due soon). She would go to the downtown hotel with the nice murals and the old-fashioned rooms. She liked the fact of its little coffee shop and the people who frequented it, who looked interesting, as if they had stories to tell, wisdom to impart. It had the added virtue of being a few blocks away from the hospital in case she began her labor and this way she could do it alone instead of being constantly hovered over, and also there'd be no ghost and so no way of knowing how she really felt about anything, which would be beneficial and would bring her, she felt sure, good luck.

It was twilight when she left, marching up the street to the bus stop. The ghost Helen stood at the window wrapped in an embroidered shawl meant for a piano. She felt the way she used to, liberated, careless, nearly beautiful. Indeed, her hair swept behind her in the autumnal breezes and on her cheek she felt a glow asserting itself, a pleasant, nostalgic sting at the corners of her eyes.

But when Guy returned she was already home again, sleeping with the dog, dreaming of a time before any of this happened, which was a time before her own life and was therefore a dream of her dying, falling away into nothingness, through a hole in the attic floor or ascending miraculously.

She woke up in the kitchen to the sound of the ghost dancing and dancing.

She knew it was happy, that somehow and in an inverse proportion its happiness signaled her own personal dismay. At the same time, she liked its happiness, its happiness seemed to be nothing so much as a displacement of her own and thus the *same* as her own. For this reason she departed to the attic taking along her usual talismans plus items from the baby's crib, the hairbrush set, the animal with chewed ears, the music box. The lovely blanket though small was adequate and the baby's pillow in its yellow linen case perfect. In the tender light which streamed over the foil-covered batting between rafters, she lulled herself into a state which verged on peacefulness and she slept most of the day and the days that followed, ate when Guy was at work, cruising through the kitchen with a plastic bag into which she plunked various cereals, figs, peaches, chocolate bars and canned sodas, read the soporific articles that collected dust at the bottom of the old trunk and returned to the main part of the house briefly at Guy's return only to show her pale and fretless face, to bid him good evening, to beg his forgiveness, before scurrying up the folding staircase once again to her little nest.

This last fact impressed Guy more than he could say, being a scientist who saw immediately the value of a behavior beyond itself: the nest made of fragments of books and those desiccated anemones from months ago, an old sweater, baby stuff. He wouldn't be surprised (and indeed was delighted to imagine) that she might pluck her own hair and weave it into the debris. Meanwhile he had his own communion with the ghost who mostly left him alone but emerged from the closet every now and again to brush its hair at the dresser. At these times he would watch the action of its hand and sigh deeply for there was something about the ghost which impressed him—its patience and sadness—and he was glad he was no longer a spectator but had been allowed into the midst of whatever mystery was being spun. This, he believed, was true science, always a matter of wonder and somehow profoundly unsolvable.

She, who had no such comforting perspective from her attic lair, continued to brood, hen-like. Sooner or later things were bound to change—for better or worse. And she would change too, as would the surrounding world, as would her memory of this particular world, which already, in imagination, had become dim and inconceivable.

As for the ghost its presence was hardly ever required. It drifted through the attic on occasion, never failing to bring with it a cooler breeze, its dreamy spiral of breath filling the eaves with mist. Then it would leave.

MONSTERS

Inexplicably, the roommate has hairy floots and a bumpy snout. Beneath her bonnet twitch the beige ears of a meadow vole with pink, waxy, alert interiors. She is not able to speak above a silvery whisper when she confronts him, hissing, You have to do something about your daughter. Each time he visits, she confronts him thus and also hisses, She calls me a fucking bitch and tells me she hates me. It is kind of mean of her, he agrees patiently. His daughter has been sick for longer than he remembers. The daughter's roommate is some kind of monster, he does not know what kind. She is humorous-looking but also a bit frightening with her floots and snout.

Try to be nicer to her, he tells his daughter, but his daughter's face hardens at the suggestion. She can't help it, he continues, Try at least not to swear or to attack her physically. This last was routine, according to the caregivers, the daughter grabbing a cane or other object and hurling it at the roommate or wheeling her own chair to the edge of the roommate's bed and menacing her. After much pleading, the daughter will promise to try to ignore the roommate, but because she has a memory deficit, she will soon forget her promise. She is brain injured, he told the roommate once. I am brain injured too, said the roommate, snout a-wobble. My brain fell out of my head. Why do you think I look like this? I know, he said (though he had no idea), And I'm so sorry.

His daughter has been sick longer than he remembers and he visits her in the facility every other day. He brings her salad and iced mochas, sometimes a t-shirt or a book. She does not remember very well, so the book will go largely unread. Perhaps the first chapter will be read over and over for the next year. At this point, the daughter is declining. This is not his word, but the word of her caregivers at the facility. *Decline*, he thinks, like the stock market. He doesn't like the word because it feels

53

euphemistic, a gentle sort of word for what is happening lately to his daughter.

Sometimes people look at the stars and marvel how far we have not come—in other words, they look and they realize that any progress from factory to grave, as it were, is less than an eyeblink compared to the progress of planetary bodies over all those millions of eons and still shining due to the mysterious business of light years. Another way of saying this is to marvel at how everything outside of our perishable selves seems to last indefinitely. When he looks at his daughter he tries to remember this—that she and he and all others have not much time on the planet, no matter how implacably constructed, and so are deeply insignificant.

"I go from city to city, from town to town," goes the song and he hums it as he drives to the facility. This time he thinks to bring the roommate a little peace offering. He does this (he admits to himself) not out of compassion but because he believes it might cut down on the complaints. The complaints knuckle him under. He has lately been in the habit of inserting his buffler so he will not feel quite so hollowed out.

He brings a floral-scented cushion for the roommate. The daughter rolls her eyes. Why her? Why always her? she asks, because she doesn't remember. She is declining, says a caregiver sorrowfully. Not only is she not remembering, she is confabulating. Now she thinks the roommate is the other daughter, the preferred sister.

Today's caregiver wears a wreath of orange labbies around her head and long black mards embossed with zanims. How clever, he says, indicating the zanims and hoping to distract her from the topic of his daughter's decline. Everything is infectious in today's world, says the caregiver. We must do our parts to curtail the spread.

"I go from city to city, from town to town, looking for a bowl of soup, looking for a dog to poke," goes the song inside of the father's head.

Usually he pushes his daughter to The Dollar Store, then to Safeway. She can have whatever she wants, he tells her. The sky's the limit. Today she is on a stretcher and possibly cannot go out, they say. He gets, No you cannot push that stretcher across the street even though it is on wheels. She is declining, she cannot hold up her head.

He takes out the buffler in order to release some of his gnarls. He remembers the daughter when she was an athlete, running cross-country into the woods where she would disappear for a little while and then reappear in front of the pack. Those moments did not require buffering and there were no gnarls building up—only, like, one glister after another. It was a veritable sea of glisters everywhere rocking and shining, the daughter running into the woods and emerging in the lead, or later on, the celebrations, the glisterous celebrations in the bright lee-pads.

Her forehead is covered with freckles—how they have persisted when all else has declined.

He smells the place where her hair stretches back from her forehead, the place where the freckles begin. Is it a nice smell? asks the daughter. It smells like you, says the father, a mixture of ruts and splay. I thought so, says the daughter. It's what I would imagine.

The roommate is neither happy nor unhappy about the gift of the cushion. Her face wears a neutral expression. What am I supposed to do with this? she hisses. Perhaps for your bed? he suggests. She waves one hairy floot. You need to help your daughter. She calls me a fucking bitch and tells me she hates me. It is a pretty cushion with mignons and bings, a little embroidered monkey swinging from a branch in the middle. Perhaps it will cheer you up, he says.

The stars. They are, after all, so far as to be nonexistent. Perhaps all things perceived at a great distance no longer exist. Only in memory do these things unreasonably persist. The insides of our minds may as well be skies filled with what is no longer in existence. When we look at the night sky, we are therefore perceiving a vast memory covered with recollections.

Imagine a mind without memory: a starless sky or a sky simply hollowed out like a feeling when overcome—or emptier.

The caregiver with the orange labbies and embossed mards is busily hooking up an apparatus called the Hoyer Lift to the daughter so that she can be transported to the toilet, set down upon it and then removed. They say that in deference to the father they will allow her to sit in a wheelchair for a short time today. Now the father can push her to Burger King for a salad and a mocha. Afterwards, they walk up and down the Safeway aisles looking for shampoo and a magazine and the daughter's head is soon resting on her own shoulder at a horrible angle. In this pose, she cannot help but stare at the rows of phosphorescent lights on the Safeway's ceiling. And this makes her say, When are we leaving?

The sky is so blue today and the clouds are noble and stately, like ships passing in front of our eyes, he remarks. They remind us, says the daughter. Of what? says the father. Oh who can remember, says the daughter.

At The Dollar Store, which is going out of business so that everything is now only fifty cents, they purchase a little figurine of a dwarf that looks as if it's made of mucus and spit. The dwarf has a very wide face and a tiny grimace which reveals just a sliver of tooth. It is so resolutely hideous that they cannot stop themselves from laughing right in the store in front of the sales clerk. Good Lord! says the daughter. When she laughs she gets very red-faced and she clenches her one good fist. She is one of those who wheezes when she laughs and now she is wheezing and wheezing at the ugly figurine. Something to remember me by, says her father, who is also laughing.

The roommate has the TV on, as usual, when they return. She is a fucking bitch and I hate her, says the daughter matter-of-factly. The TV is cranked all the way up because perhaps the roommate's meadow vole's ears, despite their alert, pink interiors, are defective. The father approaches the caregiver who is still with labbies jittering around her head, as if she were about to be attacked by wolves, he thinks unkindly. Can we get the roommate to turn down the TV a bit? No, that is not possible, says the caregiver. She has rights, too, she adds.

A buffler does not repair so much as stave. Constructed of translucent slop-jet and a series of prons and rivvels, the idea is to simulate forgetfulness. An excellent photograph might accomplish the same unless the photograph were to show the daughter having emerged victorious from the woods, a good four or five seconds ahead of her competitors, her sweet face rapt and dripping with sweat, her green shorts flashing like the neon streak of a dragonfly past the father's gaze who is beaming as she crosses the finish line and accepts a high five from her coach while still running, then looks up to catch his eye and grin.

No one ever would have predicted that her factory-made brain-box would not survive. How fragile we are! The father often thinks, thinking also, at the same time, How intrepid we are!

Before he leaves, he places the hideous dwarf figurine on his daughter's bureau and she looks at it in bewilderment, as if she has never seen it before. What in the world is that? she asks him. This is when he cradles her head in his arms and smells that lovely place where her hair meets her freckled forehead.

The TV lowered, the roommate is now snoozing into her cushion, the rattle of her monster breaths causing the embroidered monkey to somersault on the embroidered branch. Don't love her, says the daughter. Don't ever love her. At this the roommate will open one hand-slicked eye and hiss, She needs your help. YOU FUCKING BITCH! the daughter will then scream and this scream will pierce the father's heart and neatly hollow him out, despite the buffler.

"I go from city to city, town to town, looking for a soup to sip, a dog to poke, for a rock to throw and life has done me dirt, alright, life has done me dirt." The words to the song are not precisely accurate, the father knows, but they capture the defeated spirit of the time.

MOUSE CHOIR, AN OPERA

1. Today a mouse choir will perform for us Verdi's *la donna e mobile*, which means woman is fickle.

2. The mice with their weak chins and strong noses have ferreted out our desires which are otherwise secret.

3. Kafka had a habit of incorporating mice into fiction.

4. Our desires are not so extraordinary, claims Rigoletto, a grotesque dwarf.

5. Adorable in bonnets and knee socks, they approach the stage like a band of three-year-olds, uncertain of what is required, bewildered....

6. Kafka had a habit of visiting prostitutes.

7. Verdi began an affair with a soprano "at the twilight of her career."

8. They assemble in a pool of greyness.

9. There was, for example, one called Josephine, a soulful queen.

10. *Woman is fickle woman is fickle* they will soon sing, but they know not what they sing.

11. We, on the other hand, with our hidden desires, our secret yearnings...

12. How we long to be placed in another era, among a new crop of mice!

13. Before singing, it is customary to squeak a little

14. as if pumping the air out of a room.

THE COUPLE

At first Martin was with Erin, then he was with Carol, but before that he was with Melanie. After he left Carol, he went back to Erin but then he met Joan and decided to be with her instead of Erin, only he didn't tell Erin and when she found out she blamed Joan. At the time, Melanie was with Gaylord, but then Gaylord died, so she began to be with Martin since Joan was away most of the time, though she and Martin both denied they were with each other to Joan. Dana wasn't with anyone, but Martin secretly longed to be with Dana, but he wouldn't admit this to Joan. Melanie meanwhile met Luke and told Joan she would be with him for a long, long time and finally Dana met someone who kept changing his name but she seemed to be happy with him for at least a week and a half. Martin recommitted to Joan since the others were taken but Joan wasn't sure she wanted to be with anyone. Erin really wanted to be with Martin and hated Joan and Joan was tired of all the drama. She told Martin he should be with Erin and that she, Joan, would be with no one since being with no one is what she most desired since it entailed no drama. The older she got, the less tolerant she was of drama, said Joan. But Martin enjoyed drama and refused to give her up.

WRONG BODY TYPE

She said she was the wrong body type for this outfit, whereas the other one was the right body type. She herself was short-waisted and long-legged and the other was short-legged and long-waisted. Therefore, she herself could wear a jacket below the hips but the other had to beware of such jackets. In this particular case, she herself was unable to wear a blouse with a shirred bodice because the flouncing below breast-line gave her a dwarfed look which was unattractive and misleading. Because, on the whole, she was not unattractive. The other was more attractive, true, but she herself was attractive enough, especially if she wore clothes that suited her body type. Oh pass me the salt, she herself said to another person not involved, not at all involved, in this story.

THE HUG

In your acquaintance is an attractive woman who is given to lengthy and, in your opinion, unreasonable hugs. Grinding herself joyfully, bosom to bosom, this person's hug borders on hostility, you believe. No matter who you are, you get the hug. Long minutes after the hug has begun, you are released. You find it outrageous! He, on the other hand, takes pleasure from the hug. I like a person who is warm and open with their feelings, he states pointedly. And though you try to disabuse him of his opinion, observing that the nondiscriminatory hug suggests, *au contraire*, a mechanical and insincere way of relating to the world—even Hitler would get the hug! you argue—he will not be swayed.

THE EVENING VISITOR

They'd been watching TV, a show about a group of people who compete to cook the best meal for a team of judges. Just as the loser was about to be revealed, the one who'd be eliminated and sent home, the doorbell rang. Who could it be at this hour? Sam said. A murderer, Ruth said.

They peered out the window to the front stoop. No one. Some kids, probably, he said. They rang and ran. We used to do that, she said. We'd gather up dog shit in a bag and light it on fire and ring a doorbell. Then the person would come and stamp out the fire. Did you really do that? he asked. No, she said, but we did a lot of ringing and running.

Then the doorbell shrilled out in a commanding way, followed by a series of sharp slaps to the door itself, as if an emergency were in progress. Hold your horses! said Sam, turning the deadbolt.

Framed in the doorway's dark rectangle was a tall, rail-thin man wearing a bulky green coat and a wide-brimmed straw hat. He carried a large plaid suitcase covered with stickers. I wonder if I could have a word, he said. From a side pocket he produced a card that read, *Mr. Millbank, Tricks of the Trade*.

Ruth put her hand to her mouth to stifle a delighted laugh. She figured someone was pulling a prank, one of their friends. By all means, she said, gesturing elaborately to Mr. Millbank to enter their home. *Ruth*, Sam hissed under his breath. He was more prudent than she, less likely to surrender to whim. My name is Ruth, said Ruth to Mr. Millbank, and this is my boyfriend, Sam. How de do, said Millbank, who swept by them into the living room and looked around. Very nice art on the walls I see, he said.

How may we help you? asked Sam, his arms crossed tightly in front of him. He shot Ruth a dirty look and she winked at him.

Interesting phraseology, said Mr. Millbank, the offer of help, when it is I who have come to help you. He smiled. It seemed to Ruth he had more than the usual share of teeth—hundreds of tiny teeth in a wide sloppy mouth. When he removed his hat—a ridiculous hat, like the hat of a rickshaw driver or a scarecrow—an outlandish shock of red hair tumbled out and fell nearly to his waist. Oh my! said Ruth. If she'd been in a theater witnessing a performance, she couldn't have been more thrilled.

She almost clapped.

Button by button, Mr. Millbank unfastened his voluminous coat. His fingers were thick and stubby for such a tall, slim fellow and they fumbled awkwardly with the coat buttons. At last the coat fell open—two large, gray flaps framed a narrow body and gave him the look of a moth. He turned to Sam and nodded graciously. But since you ask, you may take the coat and hat.

The cooking competition was still going on. They could hear snatches of the judges' final assessment—"under-salted," "I almost threw up," "what was that brown puddle on the top?" and so on. As amused as Ruth was by their visitor, she longed to see the rest of the show; the results of the competition were for some reason meaningful to her, whereas Sam did not care so much about these shows. He felt it was not enjoyable to watch a show about food when one could not taste the food. He preferred the history channel, which Ruth dubbed The Hitler Channel. Still, in the manner of one who was doing his part in their relationship, once a week he watched the show with her, his hand resting placidly on her knee.

Ruth could not say why she liked these types of competitions as much as she did. She supposed it was because the unplanned dramas of real life fascinated her. She refused to believe these shows were fixed.

Millbank had settled himself on their leather couch, red hair spilling over his shoulders in silky, girlish waves, plaid suitcase at his feet. Without his hat and coat he was less imposing, almost frail-looking. Still he was odd, with all that hair, his face a tiny oval in the center, the cavernous mouth with its dozens of teeth. Ruth could not shake the impression that there was something insectile about him. Hoisting the suitcase to his lap, he snapped open the several latches, which produced a series of sharp, mocking cracks, like gunshots.

What have you there? asked Sam, an amused glint in his eyes. Ruth was glad to see that Sam was getting into the spirit of it.

I have knives, said Millbank, that you wouldn't believe. He removed a number of polished wooden trays from the suitcase and squatting to the ground, he laid them on the floor, end to end. Like you wouldn't believe, Millbank repeated. The trays were covered with a dark velvet-looking fabric, the kind of fabric you might see blanketing jewels in a jewelry case. Knives, repeated Sam.

The knees and elbows of the squatting Millbank jutted at sharp angles—mantis-like, in Ruth's opinion—and there might have been antennae hidden beneath that hair. She imagined such antennae creeping out unexpectedly, like worms.

Somewhat ceremoniously, he drew back the luxurious fabric from one tray. There indeed lay a gleaming row of knives, each in its narrow coffin. You're a knife salesman? said Sam, laughing now. I sell nothing, said Millbank. My business is in trade. Only barter goes into this bank, said Millbank, inexplicably tapping his head.

We don't need any knives, said Ruth coldly. It had dawned on her that this was not a prank engineered by one of their friends and she was annoyed. Sam, on the other hand, seemed to be enjoying himself.

Show me what you got, he said, pointing to the tray. All in good time, said Millbank. He made a show of revealing another tray of knives, lifting the corner of the fabric with the slightest trepidation, as if what were beneath might jump out and attack him. In this tray, the knives were larger, their blades fatter and presumably sharper; they seemed to be grinning inanely at the ceiling. No thank you, Ruth said. We have enough cutlery. Unbelievable knives, said Millbank, ignoring Ruth.

Millbank kept at these activities for a time, removing fabric from each tray, wherein the knives got successively larger, the blades thicker, longer. When it came to the last tray, he paused and surveyed his audience. Ruth was staring into space, her aggravation visible in the two vertical lines that appeared between her eyes. Sam leaned against the wall, and smiled faintly. He continued to be amused, but truth be told it was Ruth's irritation that amused him most: it served her right. She was always doing things like this, inviting strangers into the house. She had a bizarre notion of entertainment, which he'd never understood, and now she was getting her comeuppance.

Ruth was only half-listening. She had been thinking about her cooking show. There was a boy she liked who created dishes with flavored foams. He looked to be a small-boned boy with large liquid eyes behind his black-framed glasses. She imagined the foams to be like the boy— intricate, slender, dreamy. It was not true that one couldn't taste the dishes on the cooking shows.

May I present you with the *pièce de résistance*? Millbank said. With a flourish he revealed the contents of the final tray. There lay a massive knife whose blade dazzled as if lit from within. I call this knife my Sugar Momma since she's given me so much in the way of reward, said Millbank. Ruth rolled her eyes. Huh, she said.

Millbank regarded Ruth affably. Well, well, young lady, what would you say if I told you that this knife can cut glass? Ruth shrugged. She didn't know much about knives and their cutting power. You can tell me whatever you want, she said. We don't need a knife to cut glass.

Millbank grinned. It'll cut bone too, and porcelain. Why this knife could cut your toilet bowl in two! he said. We don't need knives, repeated Ruth. Her voice had taken on that flat quality which brooked no argument.

We really don't, agreed Sam. It's getting late, he added.

Millbank stood. I suppose it is, he said, clearly disappointed. The large knife, the Sugar Momma with its gleaming, luminous blade, hung slackly at his side. For a moment, he took in the pictures on the walls, pausing at the colorful acrylic of the blue gorilla over the sofa. I like that painting, he said sadly, very much. And I also like this one. He pointed to a small oil of a ballerina that Sam had acquired from a New York gallery. He'd spent most of a full month's pay on it.

You're an art lover? asked Sam, despite himself. Oh yes, said Millbank, oh yes I certainly am. I like the moderns—Klee, Klimpt, Rauschenberg, Picasso, of course, but also his countryman Juan Gris and Dalí, for fun, and Rothko, Hockney. His voice faded. The swimming pools, he said vaguely. The chapel.

Well, well, said Sam. You know your stuff apparently. There are not many of us, agreed Millbank, looking at the floor with such intensity that Sam followed his gaze to a spider making its way along a floor board.

Ruth was not a collector. Moreover, she failed to understand the mentality of collectors—a kind of greedy, grasping mentality if you asked her. Collectors and their ilk longed to gobble up the world, believed Ruth. Courtesy of Sam, she was the beneficiary of a home with fine art on the walls. Every day she could feast her eyes. To be honest, she soon grew tired of each piece. She could almost count the days until a work of art became invisible to her, though she never mentioned this to Sam.

There was the Goya intaglio from the *Capricios* on the mantel; the signed Siqueiros drawing over the bed; in the powder room, three watercolors of Parisian street scenes by Jacques Villon; a 16th century Japanese woodcut in their entryway; and more, more. For Ruth, it was as if they no longer existed.

Dimly, she heard the host of the cooking show congratulate the winner.

Millbank sniffed loudly, as though aggrieved. May I use the facilities? he inquired.

Sam led him to the small powder room off the hall. Then, by silent consensus, Sam and Ruth stood by the front door holding the big green coat and the scarecrow hat, poised to escort Millbank from their home. There they determined to stand, even while he reassembled his knives in the plaid suitcase.

Sam whispered, This is all your fault. You didn't exactly do anything to discourage him, said Ruth. He's taking a long time in there. Perhaps he's shooting drugs, offered Sam. Or pooping. Ruth laughed. Maybe he's cutting our toilet in two, wouldn't that be funny? Not so funny, said Sam, recalling that Millbank had taken the knife into the bathroom with him. He took the knife? Ruth said, horrified. Probably just afraid we'd steal his Sugar Momma. As if.

Another episode of the cooking show had begun to air; tonight's marathon would go on for hours. The slightly accented voice of the moderator could be heard, a languid, sultry voice that nevertheless had the capacity to harden when displeased by a performance or dish. Briefly, Ruth entertained the notion that the cooking show might never be over, that it would go on and on into perpetuity, that the small-boned fragile boy who moved her would continue forever to concoct his flavored foams, to present them with trembling lips to the table of judges. That no one would win or lose. What would life be like, she wondered aloud, if nothing stopped?

69

That's why I collect art, Sam said. It's eternal. Don't you see that? He contemplated trying on Millbank's coat and hat, for a joke. He thought it might make Ruth laugh. More than anything Sam was gratified by Ruth's laughter. But it would have been just his luck if Millbank emerged from the bathroom the minute he'd gotten his arm into one of the voluminous sleeves.

But Millbank didn't emerge. They waited, Sam and Ruth, until they tired of standing, at which point they resettled themselves in the living room and listened to strains of the cooking show from the sofa until finally they were drawn to the TV room in time to witness the fragile boy who made foams narrowly escape elimination. The judges were displeased, but not enough to tell him to *Pack up your knives and go home.*

This, the show's repeating mantra, suddenly struck each of them as hilariously apt. Pack up your knives and go home! shouted Ruth. Sam joined in, Pack up your goddamned knives and go home! Because Millbank had still not left the powder room. He could be on the floor, bleeding to death for all they knew. Or he might have chopped apart their toilet—two giant halves of porcelain on the bathroom floor and water everywhere.

Knock-knock, Sam said, pounding on the bathroom door. Come out come out wherever you are, said Ruth. She picked up one of the smaller knives from the array in the living room to defend herself. Pack up your fucking knives and go home, Sam was shouting. He said it again, this time shooting a gob of spit at the bathroom door. Then he kicked the door once or twice, Your fucking cocksucking knives, pack them up and GO HOME!! Your cunt-faced knives!! Ruth chimed in. Faggot, faggot, faggot! Sam was screaming and waving his arms around, in a kind of frenzied rage.

After a while he collapsed on the hall floor and Ruth bent over him. He was weeping and gasping for air, trying to scream but his voice was so hoarse that all he could manage were the words *ass-wipe* and *faggot*. His hand was clutching her arm and she had an impulse to dig into it with the knife. To carve her name deep into skin and muscle and bone.

But the moment passed. He released her arm and stood and she set the knife carefully on the hall table.

They regarded each other coolly, almost the way you'd regard a total stranger who had interrupted your evening television watching and tried to sell you something you did not want or need.

The good thing about this, said Ruth, is that we'll look back years from now and it will make us laugh. Laughs in the bank, agreed Sam.

The cooking show marathon went into a fourth and fifth hour. The fragile boy of Ruth's heart bore it bravely when, at the penultimate show, he was eliminated. As if sensing his delicacy, the judges were kind and spoke in soft, cajoling voices when they announced his failure to win the competition. You have a beautiful talent and a beautiful spirit, said the moderator in her sultry accent, but now you must leave the premises.

As for the knife salesman, he never materialized. He'd squeezed through the bathroom window, cutting an immaculate aperture in the bubbled pane (no doubt with his excellent knife) and taking with him the three Jacques Villon street scenes of Paris. In addition to the hat and coat, he'd left behind the case of knives, but these were never much good, either failing to cut smoothly or snapping off at the hilts.

10 BIRDS

1

When I woke up, birds were entering the room, their voices flutey &
sharp-witted. The pillow's fine creases had imprinted themselves on
the skin of my cheek. I checked myself for the feeling of dread. This is
like taking a temperature and involves a body scan but no instrument.
As usual, I remind myself of the bed's great comfort due to expensive
memory foam purchased to disguise lumps. Soon everything in the
world will duplicate, memory foam as hat.

2

I was struck by the presence of birds tiptoeing across the floorboards
(bedspread?). I actually despised this pillow & the way it rebounded
from my head's weight seemed to herald the dread I felt. As if we have
power to affect nothing. I scanned the room—a little light scurried up
the walls. The man beside me was dead to the world. If I had to duplicate
myself I wouldn't know where to begin but I can imagine clones walking
among us, even waking beside us.

3

The man beside me rolled over as was his custom. It was as if he were
telling me to go back to sleep. Too many birds in the room, now they were
beside me flicking their feathers. I never cared for their song which was
unmelodic but let's face it the birds were a metaphor for the dread I felt. I
scanned the back of my hand for some kind of indication that time would
heal all wounds. My pillow had slipped to the floor and with it one of the
smallest birds upon whose face I read an expression of weariness.

4

At this point, I believed things had changed places with other things.
In place of the man beside me was his pillow. This was curious because I
knew the pillow was a metaphor for weariness & the birds seemed to be
hiding. I wondered about the light, its creases within other creases felt
like one more duplication, like a memory unmoored from its moment,
a phrase that occurred to me as I regarded the man beside me. Also
there was an impression of a series of objects floating across the room.
Something melodic here.

5

Sunlight seeped through the wooden blinds & I heard the birds rattling
around in the trees. I heard the two-tone note of the mourning dove,
a sound residing in my memory & ushering in a cluster of images from
that era—brown dust of backyard, the apricot tree which someone
cut down. How the birds loved those apricots. There was another man
beside me. The walls mint green, not a good choice.

6

Dread was ushering in my body, dead to the world, as if on all four
corners the birds were bearing with me. Where had I been that such
melodies prevailed? There'd been a time, I felt certain, that duplicated
this time, but was not remembered. The two-tone notes of the
mourning dove—a cluster of mourning doves—were as ghosts, some
shadowy particle of half-tone objects that flew by too fast. I tried to
awaken the man beside me but in his place the creases on the pillow
were transferring themselves to the air, whipped up by birds' constant
feather flicking. How comfortable was the bed with its memory foam,
as memory is always a comfort, ushering in feelings of a life well-
connected & aptly metaphorized by a series of floating objects.

7

As though I had never slept at all, so stationary were the room's accouterments. The man beside me let out a groan & I knew for certain that this time was an exact duplication of another time, a time in which I'd been sleeping beside another man in a room whose walls were mint green. For a moment, then, I felt dread creeping along the pillow & imprinting itself on my cheek. I was aware of an hallucination of birds but these I knew were symptoms, not exactly metaphors, since they existed outside the window in a chorus.

8

I woke to sleeping on my hand instead of the pillow & what I'd thought were the pillow creases imprinted on my cheek was actually a map of my future, complete with luck lines & love pits. The man beside me seemed to have vanished but the memory foam held his shape like a saucer holds a cup out of which a cluster of objects might suddenly spring & proceed to float across the room. I too was thirsty. The two-tone note of my dream accompanied the light which scurried up the walls which were not mint green but interrupted by the slatted blinds through which sunlight seeped. I perceived a little cornice of dread in my body scan but I dismissed it as a shadowy column bearing the weight of memory (foam).

9

It was green & frightening. Who was I kidding, the birds had arrived & they were insistent. Although there was no instrument involved, the scan of my body proceeded as mournfully as the little two-toned notes of the mourning doves. I was searching for the man beside me, eyes closed against the light seeping through the slatted blinds, but encountered only the memory foam, the place where he'd been before he rolled over. Such melodies prevailed in a manner that came closer to a cluster of floating objects flicking against the scurried light on the walls. The birds were metaphors for ghosts & I removed my hand from beneath the creased pillow.

10

It was in this particular room & bed, in no particular order. If the man had been a bird, his voice sharp-witted, flutey instead of dead to the world. My feeling of dread so familiar it is an old friend like the light which exists in & out of creases whose creases are two-noted & definite as opposed to the shadow play of objects I made up for this occasion. The man may or may not be beautiful, the mint green walls of my past should not be inflicted on anyone & the birds have fled. In another less metaphorical sense everything duplicates & reduplicates which makes memory foam redundant & antithetical to waking at all, either beside or not beside a person who has rolled away or who has moved a pillow to replicate what may occur to him, unmoored to the moment, remote & indispensable.

SHOPPING

We are shopping and the proprietor is entertaining us with a flute.
After the flute playing, he stalks us from table to table whilst chanting.
We do our best to ignore the chanting, hovering proprietor though he
clearly wants our admiration. The chanting is very charming, very well-
executed to be sure, but we did not ask for it. We examine a Mexican
retablo replica and a Tibetan altar cloth replica and a Russian icon
replica. The man stops chanting in order to share with us the story of
his first date with his wife. They were traveling to Las Vegas and he left
his credit card in a gas station and on the same trip the hotel they were
staying in burned down and then they were stuck in a snow storm. We
believe now that the man wants to be admired for the disastrous first
date with his wife. More admiration! Again, we feel victimized since we
did not request to be amused by the tale of this man's first date with
his Brazilian (it turns out) wife. In fact, the more we peruse the items
in the man's shop—all replicas! all fakes!—the more we realize that we
want nothing from this man and that we will give him nothing—not
pity, admiration or money. In the end, though, we purchase a little box
of incense.

A THEFT

The Nanny stole a tweed suit from Banana Republic, a cashmere
sweater (pale grey, my favorite), a bite-sized digital camera, an iPod,
a sheet of checks and other things that I have not yet discovered
missing. She was a blond girl with a wandering eye, almost black in
color, an eye that rotated wildly, like a little agitated wheel in the
upper right-hand corner of her face, whenever she spoke. Because
of the eye, I was tempted not to trust her, which made me decide
especially to trust her because if we all went around suspecting a
person with disability, where would we be? The answer I now know is
that we'd be richer by almost one thousand dollars.

ON BLISS

Beautiful things occur to those who wait. I was told this as a child and I can still see laundry floating like ghosts on the line—our shirts, socks, underpants—as my mother spoke. Behind which (words, laundry) the city stationed itself, building upon building, like a mountain range.

I never wanted to be a maid. In my heart of hearts, what I wanted was music, that is to be enveloped like the saints were enveloped. The world seeming all of a sudden immensely large or small and I a perfect teardrop or grain of sand or preposition. Maybe I wanted to be a saint.

Around us were fire escapes and laundry, laundry and fire escapes, the subway sound like rockets or bombs zooming in then out of hearing. Just the way frying bacon can sound exactly like TV static or traffic like the ocean, all sounds fell into each other in the city, so that I got the idea that the essence of the world was to stir itself up like a stew.

In my heart of hearts, what I wanted was music. I played the violin, holding my bow just so, elbow out, and my teacher would say watch the ceiling! because I was tall and the instruction room was tiny. My teacher was an ex-hippie and her husband was always cooking something strange when I got there—day lily pods or lentil patties. He would bustle hungrily around the kitchen humming as I tried to get through a page of music with my teacher. I liked the fact of his bustling nearby because he was very handsome. But imagine humming when someone was trying to play the violin! I crouched as I bowed, straining toward a single spectacular pitch, high E, which I was told would vibrate the dishes in the cabinets.

I worked for an elderly man and his daughter in the upper east side. The apartment was filled with expensive paintings and "collectibles," as my mother would say, and the refrigerator regularly stocked with sheep's milk cheeses and beluga caviar and other gustatory pleasures such as Häagen-Dazs popsicles, which I gorged on compulsively after supper.

78

I gorged on whatever I could because this was the era when the things you wanted could quickly evaporate and the air bustled hungrily like the violin teacher's handsome husband. I gorged on bologna sandwiches, pizza, trout almondine, salmon en croute, choux pastries, Twinkies, Jolly Rogers, Junior Mints, Neccos, Alfredo sauce from the jar, you name it. Food was food, just as a person racing to catch a subway was not so different from the subway itself or even thoughts of the subway springing to mind from some anomalous time in the future.

I gorged on the future, dreaming it up, dismissing it, then dreaming it up again. I would be this or that. I would go here or there. My mother reminded me, "Beautiful things come to those who wait." So I waited. But it was hard in those days when nothing stood still very long. Even the billboards vanished days after being installed—a woman with a moustache of milk overtaken by an image of a telephone or a dog or a hairbrush—and the man's apartment vibrated at odd times of day as if getting ready to take off.

Through all this, my violin teacher remained almost preternaturally calm, as if history had given up on her: she wore the same jeans she wore in the 60s and the same hand-made leather sandals and she moved around her small apartment like a cat. I loved her for her silence and her disregard of trends, but I loved her husband more for his long girlish lashes and his beautiful lips and slow smile. There came a time when I would kiss and lick those lips and probe them open with the tip of my tongue, but I can't tell you that part yet.

What's important is that I practiced the violin while, at the same time, cooking for the old man and his daughter who was, I think, a nymphomaniac. Regularly, she would go off and not return for days and when she did return she would look ragged and spent. Once the buttons of her blouse had all been ripped out leaving little holes in the fabric and she was wearing a strange smile of pleasure that I recognized.

My teacher said, Watch your bowing, watch the position of your hand, your elbow, your eyes, yes watch where your eyes are watching. She spoke calmly, like a guru I once worshiped, and like him, she required the impossible. Dragging my bow across the strings felt like driving a bus full of screeching people over a series of potholes in the

79

middle of the summer. Don't worry, one out of every three adult violin players complains of the same sensation, she told me. If it weren't for her husband, I would have quit on the spot but every once in a while he'd brush up against my hips or touch my arm very lightly on the way by with his plates of food.

My employer the old man was really quite mentally ill, I believe. He complained of horrible diseases that threatened to blind him or make his limbs shrivel up. He'd spend hours in front of the mirror pinching pieces of his face, pulling out hairs with a tweezer like a woman. Then hours on the telephone with his doctor, then hours swallowing pills.

I never wanted to be a maid, but I loved to cook and cooked whatever came to mind: port wine cheddar and rhubarb pizzas, risottos with trout and nuts, lamb and mangos, strawberry chutney on a bed of candied snails. And for fun, tulips with homemade mayonnaise; sirloin and chocolate, chocolate and asparagus. In between cooking I dusted the collectibles with infinite care. Little boxes with whistles attached, or figurines in the shapes of cufflinks. Once, bending to dust a thimble-sized mirror, I saw into the world of one my nostrils to a flock of performing gymnasts, swinging from parallel bars and leaping over vaults, cheering each other on in little shrieks.

At home, my mother dusted her own collectibles which consisted of ten metal lunch boxes she'd acquired for enormous sums of money. In those precarious days we needed to believe that our pasts added up to something even though every ten years a paradigm shift occurred. The metal lunch boxes reminded my mother of her youth and how often did she tell me about the little red and black plaid one she carried off each morning with a hard-boiled egg and two cookies? How often did she mourn the passing of this or that day, like the field trip to the Empire State Building when she was in 6th grade? Looking down from the 22nd floor and feeling in her head a terrible dizziness that transformed itself to bliss. And she said that was when the strings of the world loosened, and her own strings as well, so that she floated above the city and she saw into the windows of the apartments to the people sitting with their legs up on their sofas watching TV or playing computer games. That was bliss for my mother: being able to see into people's apartments, to the programs on their TV screens.

My idea of bliss was very different. And the old man's, and his daughter's. Standing on the fire escape and shaking the lambswool duster onto the top of a bus or a person's umbrella, the city rising like a mountain range in the background, I would frequently marvel at all the varieties of bliss there must be, one for each person in the city, making millions. And it would occur to me, still shaking the duster so that my arm was beginning to ache, that some people's bliss would be more disagreeable than others' which would remind me of a newspaper story about the woman's arms that were found in the dumpster the night before. But if I closed my eyes and concentrated, the picture of the woman's arms would gradually be replaced by the eerie music of the city, like a troop of stampeding horses, racing underneath all my ideas of it, which is when the old man's daughter tapped me on the shoulder. "What if you fell?" she said, "Then you would have to sue us."

So I opened my eyes. She wore a black slip with black threads dangling from the hem and her hair was a mess. It seemed to me I hadn't seen her for days. "I'm so tired," she said. "Could you rub my back?" Her back was cold and sharp, like an object made of metal, but I did what I could, I went through the motions of massage, but really it was like massaging the back of a grill pan. That feels so good, she said and she moaned, but I didn't see what could feel good about it, which proves my point about the varieties of bliss. Then her father would emerge from his room in his bathrobe and he would say to her, Naya, what are you doing dear, put on your clothes. Then she would unfold herself from the floor, creaking like an old rusty hinge, and she would scuttle back to her room to read her pornographic magazines.

I didn't mind the man and his daughter. They were a little different, as my mother would say, but my mother was conventional. She jogged and lifted weights; she kept a dream journal; she collected lunch boxes. Who didn't know hundreds like her? Dashing to catch a train or simmering on an escalator, who didn't have their cell phones out, who hadn't checked with their astrologers, who hadn't had liposuction?

Against the conventions of the day, maybe even in spite of them, I was getting better at bowing, making daily improvements. The sound was smoother, not like a bus chugging and sputtering up Fifth Avenue, but like the inside of a tunnel during rush hour—relentless, eternal. Though I was unable to reach high E, there were consolations in the way my teacher nodded and smiled her cat's smile and in the way her husband's flirtations had advanced. Now he would stand behind me, cupping my bottom with his hands as I bowed, and his wife seemed either not to notice or not to care. She repeated her instructions: elbow out, right angle, nicely, smoothly, while he stood there looking over my shoulder at the music and whispering *cunt, fucking whore* in my ear.

I'm not an historian and it's difficult to describe the city as it was then. As a civilization we were universally aroused, universally in search of orifices or appendages. Perhaps that's why someone lopped off the woman's arms, as part of a performance piece demonstrating our impossible desires. Perhaps that's why I wanted to be a saint, as part of a performance piece demonstrating my faith that beautiful things were bound to occur.

Meanwhile, the frozen city composed the background for all our performances, like a mountain range formed by millions of years of shifting rock and evaporating oceans. At the very top of each building was apt to be someone hammering frantically on the plate glass and inside one room of every fifty, a clear-eyed, tranquil person would be plotting suicide.

Naya, said the old man, my employer, I am so tired of hearing about basketball and baseball, I am so tired of advertisements for sneakers and instant suppers, it makes me feel sick, dear. The daughter was lounging on the sofa before dinner, clipping her toenails and sending the clippings sailing through the room where they sprinkled the carpet and wedged themselves silently among the bric-a-brac. Naya, if one of those toenails scratches a Fabergé egg I will kill you, dear, said the old man. Not if I kill you first, said the daughter with a mean chuckle.

My point is that the old man and his daughter were churlish and I was no exception to this mood which permeated all of our beings in the year before our lives were set on their final courses. Who can explain how we were then? The movie theater screens featured close-ups of anguished faces and retrospectives which ached toward something all of us were forgetting rapidly. The subject matter of the world was bravery and failure, in conjunction, just as, in those days, the outer planets were all conjunct with each other for a time and were thought to presage catastrophic events. In a certain way, my life was conjunct with the violin teacher and her husband. Now we were bound up with each other and it seemed to me I was practicing our song without perfecting it. Even my teacher, who wore her preternatural calm like her Indian print dress, was beginning to fray around the edges. I saw it in the way she regarded me, sliding her eyes my way when she thought I wasn't looking. The husband raised snakes upstairs and once during a short break from my lesson, I allowed him to wind one around my neck, to flick its red tongue in the vicinity of my nipple.

My mother was the one who summed it up the best: cheap thrills. But it's what we needed to hurdle us through to the new era. Then, as we know, things became quite elevated and more reasonable. When I was a kid I buried my gold signet ring in a hole in my backyard, but now I was grown-up and had no need for further secrecy.

WISH

There was the time I got stuck in a long line of cars entering a parking garage. Impatiently, I left my car (motor still on) and went for a walk. I walked around the park, under the big shade trees. The ground, that time of year, was covered with pine needles and my feet crunched along pleasantly, enjoying themselves. In the distance I observed kids in a playground, mothers with short blond pony tails, giant purses slung over their shoulders, trees, dogs, swings, rocks, grass...

and when I returned to my car everyone was honking and screaming. Angry red-faced men were banging their fists on the hood of my car. A woman hurled groceries at my head—bag of oranges, bottle of detergent, fat roll of paper towels. Then someone pointed a gun at me. It had a rough textured handle and was quite surprisingly heavy. I knew this because I perfectly imagined its heft in my hand at which point I pulled the trigger and woke up in my own bed. Next to me, S was snoring, sound asleep. I went to his night table and removed the 1911 Colt 45 from its blue plastic case. It had a double-diamond rosewood grip, just like the gun in my dream, and it weighed about 3 pounds. *Click*, it went, when I pulled the trigger. I took aim through the window, at the sky and the leafy tree in front of the sky.

LAST QUARTET

One of us has cancer. One of us is blond. One of us is a painter. One of us is driving.

One of us has just returned from another place. Another is in considerable pain. This one makes jokes. That one laughs loudest.

She gazes out the window, thinks flat, thinks sky. Closes his eyes. Opens the peanut butter crackers. Puts out her hand.

Wishes he weren't dying and in pain. Wishes no one were dying and in pain. Narrowly misses a chair in the middle of the freeway. Says, "good steering."

Who is a curator? Who will have a round of chemo in three days? Who scrambles in her purse for her cell phone which is ringing and then stops ringing? Who takes off his hat because his head is sweating?

Returning from a place where the weather had been unpredictably warm. Thinking of a man she has begun to date. Telling a joke. Buying the first round of gas.

The surreal event of the chair on the highway, oddly upright as if someone were about to sit on it. Something derogatory about the peanut butter crackers. The entire view, his own range of vision and all that it encompasses through the plate glass windshield, reflected in his sunglasses. His knees seem to have shrunk, though this is unlikely.

Since adolescence, has worn the blue buttoned down shirt proudly, even now, as if the former century were still in full swing. Thinks it's quite possible the world will end in her lifetime, a sphere of fire biblically raining down upon. Requests an audio book. Requests a pee stop.

Imagine sitting in a chair hooked up to an IV for hours, slowly absorbing cancer-killing poison. Cows craning their necks. A daring performance piece would be to sit on the freeway chair and invite oncoming traffic to avoid killing you. Birds swelling up like music.

Every once in a while, one of us cries quietly. Having peed, another tells a joke about a man who had two sisters, one tall, one short. "Oh yeah, and they go to a bar," says a third. The fourth is a doctor.

A pleasant memory of waking in tangled blue sheets with her current lover. Wishing she could read her book without getting nauseous. Holding his hand for a long minute, then taking hers back. Swallowing another pain pill, waiting until the landscape blurs pleasantly, until his head buzzes with good will.

Has grievances. Has longings. How it will be, four days with these others? Already bored.

Hates long drives like this. Feels another should pay for gas. Doesn't drive at all. Requests the audio book.

Eats a pear. Offers the others a piece of cinnamon gum. Falls asleep. Takes off her shoes.

Thinks the audio book has a familiar plot. Still believes he can feel his knees shrinking, becoming infinitesimally smaller. Inadvertently bites the inside of her mouth while chewing gum. The landscape lusher, greener, with hazy streaks of brown in the sky.

The words *since we have learned to accept the idea that art without conventional beauty, art that is rough and strange and disturbing* make her feel dizzy and ill. A time when she gave a boy some baseball cards because he was shy. Tries not to blink for one hundred seconds and loses. Imagines he is driving a boat across an ocean and that all the other cars are sea monsters disguised as boats disguised as cars.

That tall pale boy with a Dutch last name who had no friends because he was shy and foreign. Grips the edge of the seat as the car lurches forward. We could all die any second and why not? "How about if someone else drives?"

The keeper of the snacks grabs a handful of vanilla Oreos to share. Reading *You could see a lot more if you allowed your eyes to accustom themselves to the dimness.* Seized with an improbable idea. Watching the sky, recalls that blue is conducive to creativity.

Hands over a charge card. Pumps gas. Visits the rest room, no paper towels. Purchases a candy bar.

How many more miles? Tries to sleep by resting the side of his head against the car door, daydreams. Breaks a candy bar in two and offers it around. In a certain light the road is the same non-color as the sky.

Thoughts of dying and pain have grown very small, like that tree on the edge of that hill. *You tend to forget what you are looking at is, after all, only canvas and paint.* Conceives an invention wherein fuel for a car is manufactured in a hibachi attached to the hood. Removes her glasses.

The shy foreign boy and the gift of baseball cards recollected, inexplicably. Noticing a tiny throb beginning in his left shoulder. "This audio book seems to have no plot whatsoever." Impressing the landscape upon memory: the sequence of hills and the shape of the sky, yes the sky has a shape.

What happens to memories when we die, do they float up? The daydream is sexual, but vague. Can't fall asleep. The pain in his left shoulder has moved to his neck.

If it weren't for her mother, she would never have thought to give the boy baseball cards. If the soul exists it hovers in the railroad track between lunacy and science. I wish I weren't so hungry all the time, then goes on to visualize a cake sprinkled with powdered sugar. She, the daydream, is elusive, even naked she is elusive.

In a room of many voices, like a symphony. "Where are we?" "This audio book is full of clichés." Thinking that if someone asked him right now what he was thinking he wouldn't be able to give a truthful reply.

His voice is eloquent and strong, resonant with emotion. As if he'd always known this would happen, this presentation of bad news, recalling the doctor in his green coat clicking the end of his ballpoint pen. The boy had been tall, way taller than the other 4th graders, thus ungainly, a bit monstrous. "Let's play a game," suggests one.

Repeats to himself, a passage from the dull audio book. "In the great scheme of things we are all lucky to have lived this long." "Nevertheless we hang on." "I veto the game playing because I hate car games."

Who knows who among us will die first, he reasons, stepping on the gas. "Let someone else drive, you seem tired." *But sadly, he would begin to undergo a series of bruising experiences.* "I'm starvino."

The grateful boy, a grotesque assemblage of braces and gums. Losing count of the vanilla Oreos she has shoved into her mouth. "You better start singing or you'll sink like a stone." If only they were already there or already on the way home.

One dreams up a questionnaire for the others. Unwraps another peanut butter cracker snack pack. If only he could see more cows or even just one more cow. A specific game involving letters of the alphabet.

"I ate an apple." "I blew a bubble." "I called a cat." "I drummed a let's see dromedary?"

"I eased an eel." "What is that supposed to mean?" "I fucked a fool." "I gunned a gin—and for the record I enjoyed it."

"You could have said I glazed a grape." "I held a hat." "I inked an infantry." "I jiggled a jowl."

"I knew a Korean." "I loved a laundress." "I married a monster." "A monstrous man or a monstrous model?"

"I naysayed a Nigerian." "Or a newt." "Or a Norseman." "I ogled an orange."

"That's because you're always so hungry." "Is this game fun yet?" "I ploughed a plumber." "You could always placate a pussy.".

"I quieted a quack." "I raised a ribbon." "I slapped a slug." "I tidied a tent."

"I understood an ultimatum." "I vetted a veteran." "I wangled a wrangler." "I xed out a xenophobe."

"I yanked a yacht." "I zoomed a zipper." "Or a zither." Says the last, "Shhhhhh."

The day is diminished over the rills, observes one. A blue streak as if dust, thinks another, *When despair turns phototropically to hope.* And all sounds, after a while, are one sound, thinks the third, her blond hair falling, falling in her eyes. An ending which is never, thinks the one who is about to die but doesn't quite yet die.

IN HIS WILDEST DREAMS

Although I haven't thought of him for years, I woke up thinking about him. I found myself wondering how his life was going, whether he ever married, had children, ever mended his relationship with his father, stopped drinking and/or smoking pot, still rode a motorcycle. I wondered if he ever thought of her, if in his wildest dreams he could imagine what she had come to, if he could picture her in her wheelchair, her head at that awful angle resting on her shoulder so that she has to maneuver her food awkwardly into her mouth, if he could imagine her slobbering on her shirt so that her shirts always hold traces of her last meal. Could he envision the weight she gained as a result of her medications? Had he guessed that she would become incontinent, unable to stand up on her own, and resides in a facility where they often have to restrain her because of her outbursts?

Most likely, she will have become a dim and unpleasant memory. He will be out playing in the yard with his children, his wife at the window looking fondly on and he will be throwing a ball or pushing a swing and the thought of her will never cross his mind. Or if it does, it will be like a dark cloud out of nowhere barreling across the sky. Now you see it, now you don't.

HOME IS WHERE THE HEART IS

Mary Beth

Strictly speaking, as a licensed practical nurse (LPN), it is not my job to manage the table décor, but I do it because I'm good at it. Each resident gets a rose they are welcome to pass on to their valentine-du-jour. Though *that's* kind of a sick joke, when you think about it.

Myself in a red sweater covered with pink and lavender hearts, myself in a red fascinator designed by *moi*, featuring life-sized and very realistic red hummingbird. Real enough to devour, said my husband, who is a smart a___. (To Whom It May Concern in My Creative Writing Class: A "fascinator" is a kind of hat.)

Someone suggested candies with sayings on them like "BE MINE" and "LOVE STUFF, " a sprinkling on each table like manna from the gods of love, but that person was vetoed. It is not a good thing to ply the residents with candy. Also, I can name one or two off the top of my head who have loose dentures. The dental insurance plans are not good. Once a month, the dentist arrives with his hygienist, a blond-haired girl with a wandering eye—frequently mistaken for a resident—who is perpetually chewing gum, setting a bad example for our clientele.

Today's Valentine festivities, however, do not include the dentist or his hygienist, thank the lord. Instead some families have come. Missy's mother has seen fit to join us, for example, for which we also thank the lord. Missy is prone to fits, not seizures, but spates of uncontrollable anger wherein she swears and tries to ram people with her wheelchair. Some, not all, of these meltdowns have to do with whether her mother shows up or not. Her mother: one of those senior women who tries to look younger than she is. I am not fooled, though some may be. Tonight her nails are painted black and her dyed red hair is cut in bangs across her forehead the better to hide her wrinkles. She sits next to Missy and they are hugging and kissing. Now Missy has got her mother in a headlock and is pulling her to her chest. The mother looks awkward in this arrangement, not least because her disturbing cleavage is suddenly visible, *on display for all to see*, I say out loud, only because it's true. Who wants to see that?

I see she has brought Missy a bag of gifts, one of which is the straw fedora not quite fitting Missy's big head. Missy was the victim of a brain injury and is the youngest resident. She herself claims she is the youngest by "a good seventy-five years"—quote-unquote, meaning to amuse us. Missy has no short term memory, but she is considered witty.

As a writer, I have many stories to tell about this place, not the least of which is the story of Missy and her mother. Not really a story, per se, but characters who could be in a story, when I compose the story. Our teacher reminds us (and I am remembering!) that stories have to be about something; they have to have tension. So be it. I pick up my pen.

Daniel

To steady my nerves, I nip into the Safeway, procure a pint of Jack, guzzle-up, stash in glove compartment, have second thoughts, re-stash in gig bag. Then I betake myself across the way where "one man in his time plays many parts."

Although I am the official pianist for the Immaculate Heart of Mary Elementary School, I am not a gigger. In a little while (twenty-two-and-a-half minutes) it will be just me in the spotlight, all eyes trained my way, the ring of applause, perhaps some nostalgic weeping on the part of the oldsters, people in wheelchairs like Aunt Joan. And me, singing and playing like Frank Sinatra, though Sinatra never played as far as I know.

I owe it all to Aunt Joan, she who insisted they hire me since she is living back in the past century, way far back in her poor demented brain, and, along with the shears she remembers my mother trying to stab her with when they were teenagers, is also stuck there a certain event at the community center wherein I played a solo piano piece and sang a song with the middle school orchestra.

I think a brain must be like a ginormous apartment complex you encounter in a dream where all the rooms are inside one another. To get from one room to the next are random corridors like wormholes and most of the time, knock wood, they lead you to the place you had in mind. But sometimes they don't. I'm sure my aunt had not planned to be trapped wherever she is, in that era of, god knows, Dwight D. Eisenhower, but there she is nonetheless, having somehow taken a wrong turn, wound up in a place she was not meant to return to, and fallen asleep.

Neurotransmitter. A word I like the sound of because it calls to mind an old-fashioned radio and the fatherly voice of an announcer back when life was pleasant.

There are many like my Aunt Joan in this place, this home for the whoever they call themselves these days to be politically correct, and now as I sign my name and receive my visitor's badge which I clip to my tie, I realize my hand is trembling. Nerves again. More guzzle-ups required. I am not, by nature, a performer, I am more someone who accompanies classroom after classroom of inattentive, despicable children. Who knows? this may be the beginning of a whole new me?

Missy's Mom

Oh look, we are to have entertainment, says Missy's mother to Missy. That small man with the moustache is setting his up his amplifier on the piano and look, now he's plugging in a microphone. And now, you should really turn around, he's scratching his butt, he doesn't think anyone is watching. God help us, says Missy. Despite the fedora balanced perilously on her head, she is looking especially beautiful with her hair pulled back in a black plastic claw, and wearing wooden earrings shaped like leaves. I know, says her mother, do you suppose he's mentally ill since he keeps scratching the butt? And now, he's pacing in back of the piano and let's face it there is not much room for pacing. Oh now he's sitting down and blowing into the microphone, now he's up again fiddling in that bag for something, maybe his crack pipe. Do you suppose that's a fake moustache? He can't seem to sit still—it's all the crack. I guess they've hired a tiny mentally deficient dope fiend to play the piano tonight for everyone. I myself plan to cover my ears. Shall I turn you around yet?

Missy thinks her mother is hilarious and so she laughs until her face gets very red and Missy's mom loves when that happens so she keeps it up. I dare you to go up and offer him a candy, says Missy's mom. Maybe he'll ask you on a date. I'll do it, how much will you give me, says Missy, laughing. A million billion dollars minus nine hundred ninety nine billion million.

The mom has given Missy a card, a heart-shaped box containing five chocolates and some blue earrings, as well as the fedora. The hat and the earrings are re-giftings, culled from the mom's store of possessions. The hat still had the tag and this worries the mom who thinks she may be heading into hoarderism. One of the signs of a hoarder is buying things and forgetting you bought them and/or leaving them in bags all over the house and/or not removing tags for years since never worn. Yikes. Unlikely as it is, she has a persistent fear that the hoarder TV people will one day show up with their crew and want to televise her glut of meaningless, forgotten, still tagged-and-bagged purchases.

Missy is digging into the box of five truffles, variously shaped. Mom eats two, one of which is an orange cream. The hoarding and the compulsive eating are the same pathology, she muses, as the delicious chocolate-covered orange cream fills her mouth. She wishes she had purchased a bigger box. Maybe a stop on the way home is in order. What about the piano dude, should we offer him a sweetie? says the mom. I think not, says Missy, laughing at the word "sweetie."

Mary Beth

Joan sits in her wheelchair and smiles so knowing and wise a smile that anyone would swear she were *compos mentis*. That she has not, for a long while, been *compos mentis* must be weird to those who knew her way back when, one of whom must be Daniel her nephew, who she does not recall, even though he just greeted her dutifully with a kiss on the cheek. To the kiss she gave no response except to swat peevishly at her own face, as if at a mosquito.

There's Daniel, I say, turning her chair so that she can see him setting his sheets of music on the piano. There he is! I say again, pointing. Joan looks away and down at her plate of cookies, one of which she has begun to devour methodically, nibbling around the edges like a mouse until there is nothing left but crumbs on her fingers. Not too many, dear, I say out of habit. She has snow white hair that she wears short and wavy which makes her look youthful, I always tell her. After all, she is not that old, only maybe 70. It's hard to tell with some of these, partly because they have in a way stopped advancing and so are stunted somewhere back when they were advancing. That's not a very nice way of putting it, "advancing," said my husband when I shared this theory with him. Well, he is not a trained professional. Also he has not met Missy who is forty-something and looks seventeen. The truth hurts.

Joan is giving Missy a thumbs up re the fedora. Missy nods, grateful for the compliment. They are not completely gone, this lot, thank the lord, they still have manners and some form of wherewithal, though the wherewithal part is diminished. Tragically. I think I will write about the fedora, since we are told that specifics always make a story come to life. I will call it the "jaunty fedora" and I will omit the part about it not fitting.

Oh look, dear, I say to Joan, there is your Daniel getting ready to play something. Look he is sitting on the piano bench, oh no, he is up now and getting some books to sit on. Was he always so short?

Daniel

I suppose this is to be expected, this cluster of inmates—can one say *inmates*?—, not your usual person in the street, I can tell you that. The most normal ones are that pretty blond and her boyfriend or husband with the handlebar moustache and the checkered shirt, probably related to that morbidly obese woman in the wheelchair. That woman has a mouse-colored braid running down the back of her head like Fu Manchu and a stretched unpleasant face. Her friend or sister, the highly attractive blond, holds the rose on her lap, as if she were Miss America, and turns her chair so that she is facing me, The Entertainment. Her husband or boyfriend with the handlebar moustache also turns his chair, so now that whole table is facing me and waiting for me to start. It is not time yet, I want to tell them. Look at the clock. I have been hired to play at 5:30, People, not 5:20 or 5:25. My hands are sweating.

At the next table sit two women, a very young one with a sweet face and freckles wearing a hat and a red-headed older woman who is half-naked and talking loudly as if her friend were deaf. Perhaps they are lesbians. All they do is laugh, kiss, and eat, these two, and I am keeping my fingers crossed that they will not be disruptive. Another guzzle-up of Jack would be just the thing to calm me down.

Then there's Joan and her caregiver of the evening, Mary Beth, who has the smallest eyes I've ever seen on a human and is wearing a truly hideous red sweater and some kind of coordinating headgear. Joan is eating cookies and Mary Beth is staring at me with those tiny bullet-hole eyes of hers. I'm not sure what to make of that. Perhaps she thinks I'm attractive.

96

I am attractive. There are many women, past and present, who have thought so. I have large, soulful eyes, a dapper moustache and, despite my smallish stature, I possess a good-sized schlong. The schlong has been an asset on many occasions.

Should I grow a handlebar? And purchase one of those belt buckles like the blond's husband or boyfriend? That blond is a babe and she is looking at me. You can always tell when a woman is intrigued. But it is not 5:30. The obese, incarcerated relative of the blond is shoving cake into her mouth and the husband or boyfriend of the blond is standing up showing off that belt buckle which is embossed with a pickup truck I can see from here. He is not as handsome as I am, by a long shot. His schlong is likely medium-sized.

Missy's Mom

Five foot two, eyes of blue, coochie-coochie-coochie coo, sings Missy's mom to the music. She has turned Missy around and they hold hands while singing. Missy has not been blessed with a good singing voice, but she sings loudly anyway, and the mom who believes she has been blessed with an excellent voice also sings loudly. Between us, we are wreaking havoc, says the mom. It's our favorite thing to do, agrees Missy.

That piano player plays a one-two-three-four rhythm with each song. It's annoying, says the mom. It's as if he were playing for a group of kindergarteners. Which in fact he is, says Missy, with a sly grin. Missy doesn't miss a beat either.

Missy and her mother sing *Won't You Come Home Bill Bailey* and when they get to the part about the fine-toothed comb, Missy's mom interjects: Do you suppose Bill Bailey had lice? Missy laughs.

They are always laughing because Missy's mom believes that the more they laugh they more they have a shot at staving off their sorrow, which is a deep well. A Deep Well of Sorrow is how Missy's mom expresses it. During most days, she repeats this phrase compulsively, thinking that to name it A Deep Well of Sorrow will have the effect of making the well of sorrow less deep or less sorrowful. Missy who will not remember that her mother visited. Missy who can no longer write her name.

Mary Beth

Daniel is in full swing, pounding out the oldies but goodies. "Take Me Out to the Ball Game," at the moment. Joan smiling, Ray tapping the side of his nose with one finger, fat Pamela rocking in her chair. Missy and her mom screaming *I don't care if I ever come back* and some of us would like to tell them to put a sock in it, if you know that expression. My husband says it sometimes: Put a sock in it! As if I have extra socks around to stuff into my own mouth. Ha ha.

My husband: he is home at the moment parked in front of *Law and Order*, as is his wont. I hate that show. I hate that skinny girl and I hate her bald-headed partner and the fact that they all talk in the same gloomy voice. What's so hot about real life? I want to say. But then I remember where I'm coming from, this place and its one-card-short-of-a-full-deck population. I can just hear him saying, That's not a very kind way of putting it. Mr. Law and Order. But I am a writer. We have to be honest.

Wake up, Joan, I say, because now her head has fallen forward and she's closing her eyes. Say what you want, but in this world, in the world I mostly inhabit, which is here in this place because my shifts are long, people do more or less exactly what they feel like doing, which I admire. Wake up, dear, I say anyway, and I shake her shoulder.

Daniel

Blue Moon/ You saw me standing alone/ without a dream in my heart/ without a love of my own. I am in splendid voice tonight, if I do say so.

I aim my words at the blond woman who has begun to finger her rose, tearing at the outer petals. The only drawback is that my sheets of music are in keys for the children at Immaculate Heart of Mary and so a few times I am unable to hit a note. What do they want for $35?

That rose must be slowly dying is the thought that occurs to me in the middle of the song. This is such a surprising and unwelcome idea that I stop singing and let the piano take over. We are all dying. The rose is just a manifestation of what's happening every second to me you everyone. I am sweating now on the forehead.

The husband or boyfriend or whoever he is and his blond are having a conversation and laughing with their heads together and for a minute I think they're laughing at me. At the next table the lesbian couple are singing loudly, even though I myself have stopped singing. Those two know all the words, *without a dream in my heart, without a love of my own.* There's a part of me, if I'm honest, that would like to smash their homosexual heads together until they crack like eggs and all their brain goo spills out over their clothes but since, along with the rest of us, they are doomed anyway I don't bother overmuch with this fantasy, admittedly morbid.

Daniel, why are you so morbid? I can hear my mother saying. Because I've always had a morbid streak. Perhaps that is why I don't have a girlfriend. Correction: I have had very successful sexual intercourse from time to time but those girlfriends have fallen off. People tend to fall off you, Daniel, I can hear my mother say. My mother: Dead. Aunt Joan: Bonkers. Who's falling off now, Ma?

Missy's Mom

In her real life, her life away from Missy, Missy's mother is not nearly so cheerful and funny. Why is that? In truth, being with Missy wears her out. Keeping Missy laughing wears her out. At home, Missy's mom collapses onto her bed, exhausted as if after a performance. She doesn't even take off her shoes. But here, waging war with the Deep Well of Sorrow (DWS), in the trenches with it, so to speak, and armed to the teeth, she is genuinely happy. The sweet chorus of freckles on Missy's shoulders makes her happy and holding Missy's bad hand—they call it the bad hand because it's paralyzed—makes her happy. The bad hand is warm and soft, as opposed to the good hand, which is damp. In the past, before the accident, Missy's hands were always clammy and Missy's mom would tell her they felt nasty, even as she held them. They always held hands, those two. Before and after, the handholding persisted. Persists.

Well, what do you think? Missy's mom asks Missy. Boyfriend material or not? Not, says Missy. I don't like a man with a moustache. But such sprightly playing would be a plus, no? I think he's more your type, says Missy, laughing. You could drown him out with your stupendous voice. Bitch, says Missy's mom.

For dinner, Missy has ordered her mom a piece of salmon and herself some chicken cordon bleu. The cordon blue looks like a kitchen sponge and the salmon like a club foot garbed in a soiled athletic sock. I think possibly the chef has been overly ambitious, says the mom. Oh eat it and shut up, says Missy affably.

At home, Missy's mom subsists on rye toast and candies. It is the DWS, she tells herself. Her shopping may also be due to the DWS. She shops as if in a dream, casting about in stores for something to take home, speeding through aisles with her cart, as if she were a participant in that TV contest where whoever stuffs her cart with the most things in twenty minutes wins a prize. Only the really repellent item is off-limits, everything else is fair game: potholders, cans of ginger snaps, tee shirts with glitter, high-heel sandals she will never ever wear. Ditto the coral lipstick and the violet eye shadow, the rum balls (hates rum), the yellow patent leather overnight bag—how cute is that?—but she never goes anywhere except to visit Missy or to meet Missy somewhere for an outing.

Mary Beth

At the next table Missy's mom is poking at her food with her fork as if it were a dead animal. Well I guess it is a dead animal, but geez, we do try our best here and we don't need some smarty pants looking down her nose at what we try our best to do for them and theirs. Perfectly good salmon with hollandaise, you couldn't do any better at the Olive Garden.

Of course Pamela consumes all. Her own cordon bleu as well as her sister's salmon. Pamela is on a restricted diet but she finds ways around it, goes off next door to the Safeway and stockpiles cookies and cupcakes in her underwear drawer. Do not think we don't know this, Pamela. Missy is not allowed to go to the Safeway unaccompanied. When her mother comes, off they go together, but alone she is prone to wander and forget on account of her short term memory deficit. We've installed an alarm on her chair in case she gets it into her head to go to the Safeway unattended, but she hates the alarm and sometimes the alarm is the signal for Missy to have a meltdown. You learn all the ins and outs of these people, all the ups and downs of their idiosyncrasies and moods and toileting habits. Which I am planning to incorporate into a funny story entitled "Get Me Off this F___king Toilet," which is an actual quote from Missy.

Just now Joan lurches in her chair and lets out one of her famous moans. I can see it has made Daniel stumble on the piano keys. He looks up and blinks his eyes a few times, then stops playing, mops his forehead with a handkerchief. I'm thinking he is probably hungry and maybe I should order him up a plate of food, he might want to eat a snack before going on since he is sweating a little, maybe feeling faint from lack of food. And all around him people eating and sawing their chicken cordon bleu and licking up the hollandaise on the salmon. Must be hell for him. I am like that. I feel for others.

But when I go up he says no, no food, but wants to know, in re to the hummingbird in my fascinator, is that a real stuffed bird? Then requests a bathroom break.

Daniel

In the stall I remove the Jack from gig bag and guzzle up. Burns going down and if I'm honest I have to admit that even at the Immaculate Heart of Mary Elementary School, I sometimes nip into the Boys for a guzzle up. It is calming to me. The children are often raucous, which gets on my nerves, but here with this brood, who are not raucous, the problem is having to look around, having to fill up eyes with the spectacle of inmates. Not big-eyed second graders with hair plastered on foreheads and chirpy voices who when you say shut up you could hear pins drop, but hunched over and moaning fatties or crazies, staring into space, or eating with hands, thumping on table out of time with music or because requiring more food, it's hard to say which and to say shut up to these.

An additional guzzle-up of Jack, oh yes, and now in the mirror I admire my moustache and am glad again for choosing to sprout one, which was not always the case. Without a moustache I am less attractive there being a lack of upper lip, as my mother often informed me. No upper lip just like your dad, true, gave me a look that made people go off me.

I am already planning my finale of songs to include *I Wish You Love* and *Moon River* and *Old Black Joe* for the African Americans in the audience. But no *My Funny Valentine*, since I don't know that one, sad but true.

Missy's Mom

Missy's mom leans over and asks if she has to pee because just yesterday there was an incident. I'm wearing a brief, Missy whispers to her mom.

Missy was wearing a brief yesterday, too, and they were at the nail salon run by the Asian women who had always been so kind to them. Always holding the door so Missy's mom could push Missy inside, always allowing Mom to hold Missy's bad hand open for the polish, which was hard on the mom's back having to bend over Missy's shoulder and forcing the bad hand open and holding it still for what felt like an eternity so the polish would not get ruined. But this day, yesterday, in the middle of the aforementioned proceedings, appeared a puddle under Missy's wheelchair and the Asian ladies normally so kind and friendly, became suddenly distressed and horrified. And Missy's mom ran to fetch paper towels out of the ladies' room dispenser but the handful of thin paper towels were no match for the steaming puddle of pee that had poured from Missy onto the floor. So to no avail did Missy's mom on hands and knees in front of other nail customers try to swab up Missy's pee, hands getting all full of pee. Missy saying sorry sorry to everyone, and everyone, meaning the Asian ladies, saying nothing but becoming in the face more and more frozen-looking, the nail operation halted, the implements gathered up, the little bowl of warm water with the glass balls in it taken to the sink, etc.

The Asian ladies now making a motion with their hands, as if wafting a stray dog out into the street from whence it came, at the same time holding the door for Missy and her mom to leave. We get mop, you go, one whispered to the mom and this one smiled showing all her teeth, like a jackal, thought the mom. Sorry, said the mom again, pushing Missy outside. Sorry, said Missy again. And Missy all wet down the front of her pink slacks and the mom put her own jacket on Missy's lap to hide the mess.

Once in the parking lot and waiting for Handicar, Missy has already forgotten the episode, the Asian ladies, even her incomplete and ruined lavender manicure strikes her as perhaps something she chose for effect. The mom, on the other hand, feels the DWS rising up and, as soon as the Handicar has fetched Missy, she plans to appease severely rising DWS by cruising down the aisles of Ross Dress for Less.

And just then they see in the distance an old friend wearing a straw fedora, not unlike the one fruitlessly occupying a shelf in Missy's mom's closet. And because Missy's long term memory has not been affected by her accident, she cries, Robert!—so overjoyed to see him that her eyes brim with tears. I like your hat! And Robert kisses each of them on their cheeks and they all chat as they wait for Handicar, Missy still with the mom's jacket covering the wet spot on her pants.

Where are you living now, Sweetheart? An innocent enough question posed to Missy by Robert. And Missy, who can't remember that she peed on the floor of the nail salon or the look on the Asian ladies' faces or her own repeated heartfelt apologies or why in the world she is holding her mom's jacket on her lap, Missy will quip, deadpan: *At a resort.*

THE CANCER CARD

Because he believed they were not entitled to sleep in, the houseguest blared the TV at eight in the morning. Tom plunged his head under the pillow. Next to him, Diana drooled.

She wouldn't believe she did this routinely, but she did this routinely. Crammed into her mouth a horrible plastic thing she called an "appliance" so she wouldn't grind her teeth and wake up with a headache he'd have to hear about all day. He held the appliance responsible for the drooling. Also, it set her mouth at a ghastly angle, like a zombie on *The Walking Dead*, and the zombie-like drool was disgusting, long strings of it puddling into the bed linen.

If only to appall Diane, who was nothing if not vain, he considered videoing the whole operation.

He had reached the sadly declining mid 60s, where life had begun to feel like a zero-sum game. Each sweetness speedily countered by an equivalent bitterness. Even before he hoisted himself from bed and toe-groped his slippers on the floor, before he peed and weighed himself on the high-tech digital scale he'd had installed in his bedroom (Diane said it looked like a kidney dialysis machine, though she'd never seen a dialysis machine), before he brushed his teeth and padded into the kitchen to fire up his expensive coffee machine, he could count on ten fingers the things that were at this moment annoying him.

Of these, the houseguest took first place. Cranking up the TV sound in the early a.m. was not acceptable. But the houseguest had cancer (Diane needlessly reminded him) and so they were banned from saying anything. This put a strain on everyone involved.

Playing the cancer card, Diane had said. I think that's what it's called.

I get it, Tom had snapped. But I don't have to like it.

Nearing the kitchen and his beloved Magnifica, purchased at

105

Costco for 400 dollars (as opposed to the 600 dollars William Sonoma charged), he was able to discern among the decibels a chirpy female interacting with a hearty male. Irony was involved. Audience laughter. One thought of a lurid sky, the sun ablaze in it, a thought intended for later in the day.

The houseguest had fallen asleep in a chair, his grizzled chin slumped into his clavicle, nodding out. His hair was sparse at the crown. Not even a combover could remedy that situation.

Still nodding, the houseguest thrust out his hand. Coffee? he inquired. The houseguest had expectations. Coffee. A sweet roll. Brought to him, silver platter-wise.

Since the cancer, he'd become addicted to sugar and oxycodone, not to mention the nicotine. He smoked outside in the vicinity of Maryann the tortoise, adding to Tom's worries about the creature.

Those tortoises live for hundreds of years, proclaimed the houseguest, whose name was Mac, a little secondhand smoke won't kill that one.

The Magnifica rumbled to life; like a wild animal growling and wheezing, as if to clear its enormous lungs, it ground up the beans noisily and spat out a perfect cup of coffee, according to Tom. Mac was not so sure. He preferred drip, he'd told Tom more than once.

Drip is more genteel, agreed Diane, who loathed the Magnifica.

Outside the usual beautiful weather prevailed. Odd how this fact could dampen one's enthusiasm for life, Tom reflected. Every day, the same, sunny, blue, a few breezes rustling in the palms, the swimming pool awash with sparkles. Tucson, Arizona. Who wouldn't want to visit their old childhood friend a few times a winter?

But to Tom, this perfection of climate exemplified the bitterness cancelling out the pleasure. Would he rather be in the snow and below zero temps of the northeast? No. But so much sameness was depressing, as if he were one of those bugs frozen in a teardrop of amber. All very nice unless you were the bug.

Diane arrived disheveled but, minus the appliance, a little more like a human woman. She wore flannel pajamas with a bacon-and-egg motif, her hair still in messy braids from the previous night when they'd gone to a rodeo day party at a friend's. The rodeo provided an annual excuse for a party and the guests wore cowboy hats and jeans, even bolo ties and boots. Tom had never been to the rodeo itself. He imagined cowboys with ropes and steers dipping their horns, probably confusing it with a bullfight. There was a time when he might have been interested in such a spectacle, but he never seemed to get himself there. Now that time was past.

There are two types of people, he'd recently explained to Diane and Mac, those who try to cram everything in when they get old and those who are contented to sit back and smell the coffee. I'm that latter type.

You mean the *roses*, Mac had said. It's *wake up* and smell the *coffee*, it's *stop* and smell the *roses*.

Oh thank you so much for the info, Mac, no one said.

Now Diane pointed to the back of Mac's head and made a face. They had both grown weary of Mac. Since his cancer diagnosis, Tom and Diane had been tasked with providing him with quality respite care: time in the sun, homemade meals, flat screen TV. Supposedly in remission, he couldn't seem to shake a sense that he was going to die very soon anyway.

He pops those oxys like Neccos, Diane observed, a Necco lover herself. Hundreds of oxys in a baggie graced the guest bathroom counter. Tom was always tempted to try one.

Go ahead, knock yourself out, Mac had offered, employing his maddening intonation. This was when he allowed the ends of his sentences to trail off plaintively, too exhausted to utter another syllable, thereby establishing himself worthy of pity.

Diane took her coffee out back. I think I'll go hang with Maryann, she said, which was a joke since she was fairly indifferent to the tortoise.

That tortoise gets all the love it needs, she pointed out in her own defense.

It's true, Tom fretted about the tortoise and hoarded treats for her. Last week he'd placed a bright hibiscus flower at the mouth of her den, like a lover.

You are an unusual man, it's like lavishing attention on a rock, was all Diane said.

You're unkind because you're jealous, he'd said and she'd said, Why would I be jealous of a rock?

I know you.

Every time he said it, he wondered if it were true. Did he know Diane? Did anyone know anyone?

When he and Mac were kids they did everything together. Both oddballs, they'd expended their boy energies on manufacturing public pranks, often involving explosives and occasionally the police. The prank Tom liked best to recall was the time they'd stuffed Tom's father's clothes with newspapers and hung their dummy from a string going across a busy street. One of them screamed while the other one manipulated the string. Tom never remembers who did what and Mac doesn't remember the incident at all.

Out in the sun, adamant even at this hour, Diane is reclining on the blue chaise, her wrinkles stamped furiously into her skin. "Ravaged" is the word that comes to Tom's mind. She was once so beautiful, he thinks, wistful. Or was she?—actually, not exactly beautiful, but rather approaching beauty, coming right up to its bright edge before sharply veering off somewhere. A little too expressive, perhaps, too given to the easy grimace or the unseemly laugh. It was as if, he realized with a start, she'd always been drooling.

Hi, she said, glancing up, raising her coffee cup.

Have you seen Maryann? Tom slid the screen closed and squinted up at the sky, as if he might spot the tortoise traversing a cloud.

Not hide nor hair, if that's not a cruel way of putting it.

She must be somewhere. Probably behind the bamboo.

How's Mac?

No idea. Sleeping.

And you?

I've been thinking about terrorists, he said. Which wasn't true. Terrorists had only just occurred to him. In his mind's eye they wore cartoon helmets and carried swords. Maybe he'd dreamt about them. He'd been dreaming lately—weird dreams having to do with captivity or of running in molasses and never getting anywhere, which amounts to the same thing as captivity.

Do you fear we'll be attacked? wondered Diane. Or is this a poorly disguised fear of death?

I don't know. They just popped into my mind, truth be told. Wearing knight-of-armor hats with visors. I think I should probably make eggs for Mac. He ate nothing last night.

He hated the food. He hated the party. Not that I blame him. All those people? What does one find to say beyond the initial blah blah blahs?

Mac wanted to go home instantly, which was irritating.

No shame in his game. We had to hop to or else.

He was always that way.

You're the one who likes to schmooze.

Not as much any more.

They looked ahead at the palm tree rustling over the pool. Tom thought, This should really be the life. If only it were. In the pool water, oval reflections of branch and sky. What could be more glorious when the rest of the world was freezing?

Behind a mound of oleander, Maryann allowed herself to be seen, her dome glistening, floating almost.

There you are!

Now, finally, you are joyful, remarked Diane.

Is that a problem?

Not at all—it's nice. Who's going to make the eggs, me or you?

The screen door scraped open and Mac appeared with a platter. Deviled eggs. I made them last night at three in the morning.

Diane widened her eyes. The fruits of insomnia?

If you can call it that.

The eggs had been arranged on an oval platter, in rows. Little white boats overfilled with yellow mush.

Nice, said Tom, who'd risen to consort with Maryann.

It is nice, said Diane, popping one into her mouth. Thanks.

De nada, Señora, said Mac who had been taking advanced Spanish. He was the type of dying person who wanted to travel the world, hang out at cafes with beautiful Spanish girls before he kicked the bucket. When he wasn't playing the cancer card, there was something courtly and adventuresome about him. Though he tried too hard to be droll, in Diane's opinion.

Tom was feeding Maryann a sprig of bok choy. She came right up to his hand, her reptilian mouth agape. Diane had eaten two eggs, he noted. She could never seem to stop consuming, though she wasn't very fat. Mac set his egg platter on the pool decking and stuck a bare foot in the water.

High in a tree some kind of large bird was making a racket and they all looked up. One efficient flap of the wings and it clattered away with a screaming bunch of feathers in its mouth.

The grim reaper, noted Diane.

Actually, that was a peregrine falcon, Mac informed them. They feed on small-to-medium sized birds and winter in the milder climates. Probably came down from the Rockies—they have a huge wingspan—

Oh be quiet Mac, said Diane, sharper than she intended. You sound like a Wikipedia entry.

Mac emitted a patient sigh.

The eggs were good, despite their slovenly presentation. Diane praised them to make up for her meanness.

Have another, Mac said. He'd propped a skinny left leg on the deck, the right one still splashing around, making blue circles in the pool. In the laconic wake of Mary Ann, Tom disappeared into a clump of bamboo and emerged seconds later, smiling, shaking his head.

What? Diane shaded her eyes with a hand.

But Tom declined to respond.

Through her fingers she spotted a monstrous thing swooping down, the falcon who'd returned and decided to settle on the far wall and take in the human spectacle. For a few breathtaking minutes, it sat there, stock still, as if for a portrait.

Later, they decided that the bird had possessed an artificial quality, like a plaster yard ornament purchased at The Home Depot, the feathers of its wings precisely, unconvincingly delineated, factory-made—as if it might shatter if it fell from the ledge.

PETE, WASTE LAB TECHNICIAN

Sometimes when late at night I think I see someone out of the corner of my eye, it is really only one of those roving shadows. They rove up on a wall or behind me when I am pushing an empty gurney into the Waste Lab. I do not know why it is called the Waste Lab.

I am really not afraid of anything.

When I was small, for a short time, buttons frightened me.

The gurneys have a peculiar smell, hard to describe.

I am not really sure what I should tell you about myself. The roving shadows are what come to mind because they are really so startling and mysterious, but there is also a cafeteria which at night is inhabited by a number of talkative zombies. They call themselves the Undead (predictably). And they jabber. Blah blah. They do not eat much, mainly the candy bars and juice boxes. I have discovered that they don't like meat, which seems strange to me.

Strictly speaking, I am not in charge of the Waste Lab. If you care to know what the Waste Lab looks like there are three boxy windows up very high which require a device with a hook for opening, beneath which there are the walls with all the gurneys pushed up against them. That leaves a space in the middle of the room which I enjoy traversing. The floor is golden, as is the entire floor of this building.

Have I mentioned that those gurneys really stink?

It is odd that through the Waste Lab windows which are up very high the view is always the same—night or day, it is as if a sheet of white paper occupies the space outside each window so that one has the impression of glowing blankness, of there being no world at all on the other side of the windows of this building much less the world of Why Not, Arizona, with its perfectly restored vintage fire engine, adult movie theater and my mother's Gift Shoppe, to name three things cherished by me.

You might deduce that zombies have something to do with the roving shadows. But even zombies cannot be in two places at once. The zombies, as previously stated, are in the cafeteria—all twenty, I counted—and here right outside the waste lab are the usual crop of shadows doing their usual roving up and down the walls and stretching and shrinking along the golden floors as is their wont and occasionally folding into little envelope-sized packages or splitting in twos and veering off in different directions and snaking down opposite corridors.

Perhaps meat reminds the zombies of their own lost and mostly forgotten bodies. Their own disintegrating bodies which are kept at the Why Not Wondrous Peace and Light Haven which is also a dog and cat burial ground.

I prefer the words "burial grounds" to the word "cemetery."

One of the zombies, coincidentally, is called Pete also. He usually sits alone at one of the orange tables next to the kitchen door over by the window. In the cafeteria, the windows are filled with heavy black rectangles at this time of day. Once in a while one of the roving shadows streaks across and if you didn't know better you would think it was a tree.

More than once I have attempted to approach Pete for conversation. Of all the chattering zombies he is the quietest, but still he jabbers quietly to himself. They cannot help their jabbering, it is some kind of condition, probably, that they have to put up with as zombies.

Other than the gurneys there are large plastic barrels in the Waste Lab, which they say are filled with eyes. Hard to believe, and I never checked. Though most things do not frighten me, I would not like to look into a barrel of eyes. Don't ask me why.

Pete jabbers mostly about physics. E equals em-cee squared type-of-thing. Archimedes' experiments with buoyancy; Isaac Newton and his various theories of gravity and planetary orbiting. Pete, I said to him once, do you think the elliptical orbiting of ideas is a *replica* of the elliptical orbiting of the planets? In other words, I said, still arguing with Pete, who was gazing into one of the thick black rectangles that occupy the cafeteria window frames and moving his lips very slowly, not chewing his Starburst but jabbering, could it be that we are ourselves *replica* universes and that, for example, Why Not, Arizona, is a *replica* of the Milky Way so that, in conclusion, might we say that each of us is a *replica* of the Why Not, Arizona, and vice versa? Sometimes I blow my own mind.

The other zombies sit in clumps along the side wall away from the windows and near the machines. I have never seen an animal—dog or cat—zombie and I hope I do not.

My mother, who is no longer alive, did once own a business called The Gift Shoppe which is also no longer alive, so to speak, having been appropriated by a company whose team of grinning sales people are always dressed in orange jackets. I have no idea what kind of business is conducted there. In my mother's day, gifts were sold. Now, who knows?

The waste room has fat white hoses coiled against the ceiling. Strange but true. I have often been tempted to ask Mr. M_____ the purpose of the hoses and why, of all places, they reside on the ceiling of the waste lab, but Mr. M_____ never seems inclined to converse. I only ever meet him when he is leaving the building and I am entering it and at these times he averts his eyes and hustles himself into a white Chevrolet.

I don't know how helpful this has been. I am who I am. The zombies come and go; they can be relied on to clean up after themselves—candy wrappers in the trash, chairs carefully replaced on top of tables. The roving shadows continue to mystify with their irrational movement, but I am accustomed to The Mysterious, it does not frighten me. I recently remarked to Pete that we are all enshrouded by mystery and walk around in its fog. Who is Mr. M_____ exactly and where does the white Chevrolet take him? What product is so important that six orange-jacketed sales people must overtake a nice Gift Shoppe? What about those hoses in the waste lab? The smell of the gurneys? The zombies and their dislike of meat? All mysteries that, as far as I can tell, will never be satisfactorily revealed.

OUR WAY TO THE HIGHWAY

whose surface is covered with sparkling stones in the sunlight but after dark is dog-colored (old, brown), up ahead a very slight shimmer, just the road's flatness (mirage), invisible in the evening, just empty black space (invisibility squared) since there are no lights unless there is a moon with a moon the road going & going on, about four or five miles or billboards you'll have to exit & once at the exit you will come to a stop light near a CVS & across from a Burger King which are our only reliable landmarks these days (think about it) along with the pancake place whose name I can't remember offhand though it seems to me the logo is gold-colored (gold syrup cascading down a stack of pancakes??)

take a right and continue up the road which is two-laned, pole-flanked (haze-filled) you will notice a shop that has a life-sized horse out in front with a real saddle made of leather which sometimes constitutes a photo-op for parents traveling with little children who are boosted onto the saddle & made to pose for photographs & often these little children get very frightened because the horse is so gigantic & in the photographs they (kids) are often screaming but the parents are very passionately intent on capturing this moment in time when the child is a certain small size having been boosted onto a frighteningly large horse a moment that is visualized in the album along with other memorable moments sometimes involving tears sometimes not

you will also pass a sort of shallow ditch along the side of the road (on the right) where once a group of college kids turned over their car & one of them died it was the night of graduation & it was a tragic event for the whole town & so the ditch has never been filled up (in) (erased) but left to be there just the way it is with a few roadside crosses flowers painted around which are visible on the far side of the ditch the crosses commemorating the lives of those college kids who in real life were not all that memorable or even kind one once tortured a teenaged boy who happened to have a slight handicap & another date-raped a girl traumatized her for life but they are all dead now one wants to say thank goodness but out of respect for their parents we'll say rest in peace & also keep going it's never a good idea to stop at a roadside grave even one with a nice cross & flowers keep going & you will come to a hill there is nothing to do (?) but go up it and you may have to shift gears since it is very steep but you want to make good time (otherwise you would have chosen the scenic route) so you keep going possibly you're already downshifting

& it's also a good idea to turn down your radio which is a distraction on a hill of this nature very uncommonly steep (inclining) & so you will keep plowing on up it & downshifting if need be to second & even first gear & creeping along it may strike you as ironic that the neighbor cows are lumbering out of their grazing fields & are jogging alongside your car & passing your car as if they were racing you some of them circling back to give you superior looks then waddling ahead again they always do this which will give you some idea of how steep the hill is it's a wonder the cows don't slide down backwards they are such clumsy creatures there is a story possibly apocryphal about those cows swarming a vw bug one time & the poor passengers were literally trampled to death & the car was battered beyond recognition it looked more like a blown up daycare center than a car

speaking of which if you get through the cows there is the daycare center up ahead & to your left a cute sign swinging on hinges makes this slightly annoying sound (glitch glitch) but still the kids are so adorable no one gets too angry except this one poor man (long ago) who suffered from obsessive-compulsive disorder & the sound of the sign creaking on hinges was more than he could bear so he quietly stole into the daycare center & captured one of the teachers & the most adorable of the children & forced them to commit unspeakable acts on his person until someone took the sign down but this was temporary & as soon as the man was carted off to the lunatic asylum for the criminally insane the sign was rehung & now you will see it up ahead where it casts a very nice, swaying shadow on the asphalt over which it swings in a desultory summer-day kind of attitude if a sign can be said to have attitude but pass the sign it need not concern you overmuch the children are all safe these days

except for the adorable one who was violated by the poor
obsessive-compulsive man who didn't know any better & that child
is now a grown-up living in the back of the daycare center with his
cat which is really a small puma disguised as a cat & which would just
as soon tear out your heart as bare its fangs at you & actually it does
neither because you will keep going & not entangle yourself where you
clearly don't belong with either the poor adorable violated boy turned
adult nor with his puma/cat who sometimes prowls about the grounds
of the daycare center & injures the children but this is something you
really don't need to know as you are climbing the hill there are black-
eyed Susans there are jack-in-the-pulpits you don't need to know about
the various accidents of every living thing after all the world is violent &
also peaceful there are pine trees in the distance a stand of pines there
are two blackbirds on a telephone wire but these are generally unreliable
landmarks

keep climbing (huff puff) & then finally at the top you will
come to a busy intersection just when you were expecting wilderness
on the northwest corner is a pizza place with some letters missing from
the sign so that it says IZ & on the southwest is a gas station with two
dangerous looking scarred & hooded men next to the gas dispensers
wielding guns & on the northeast corner is among other things a shop
that sells notions like buttons & once someone asked if they sold savory
or unsavory notions which I thought very funny (ha) but there is no one
there at the moment it is very quiet & dead-looking the notion shop
is without any notion at all it seems (another joke) & so you must not
pay any attention at all to the group of lepers that are chatting on the
porch of the notion shop because they are essentially harmless (really it
is not contagious) though it may give you pause that one of the lepers
ate his own daughter (in infancy—his eyesight was compromised by
the disease) but no more need be said about that essentially sad tale
& no one's fault really though not long after the mother hung herself
from a tree branch so inexpertly that she failed to die & lives now with
her head permanently off-kilter & her neck at such an odd angle that in
order to see anything straight-on she has to place herself in a vise & get
her leper husband to turn a knob

118

    & on the southwest is nothing at all it is as blank as any blank
they ask you to fill on a test that will determine if you will be going
forward or staying where you were—exactly where you were or had
been or will be, you beautiful traveling thing, you cog, you wheel, you
worm, you mosquito, who knows where you will wind up

STILL LIFE

A man told me there was nothing he would rather keep noticing—and he pointed to the spaces between palm fronds, chinks of turquoise and a few clouds. Just now, into this recollection, wanders an egg on a green dish.

L

I saw L today looking a little beleaguered and I said, How're you doing,
L? and he said, Hanging in there and I thought, Wait, maybe L's look
has to do with illness. I hadn't seen L in a while. Previously he had been
rather cheerful in demeanor, always smiling. Now it seemed there was
something not right with his mouth, as if part of it were paralyzed
and/or he was in pain from his jaw or neck. Perhaps L had been to the
dentist is all, I thought, but then why did he say Hanging in there as if
I'd know he'd been to the dentist? I hadn't seen L in months, why would
I keep track of his dental appointments? No, a person would only say
Hanging in there with that world-weary inflection, in combination with
a heavy sigh, all the while avoiding eye contact and seeming annoyed—
who wouldn't be?—if he had some chronic bad condition that everyone
knew about, except me. I wanted to say, I'm sorry, I had no idea, but
what if I were wrong and it was the dentist after all? On the other hand,
L was an older gay man and so immediately and in retrospect I thought
AIDS. But why stereotype, it could have just as easily been cancer and
really what I should have said was, What's going on? A polite, logical
follow-up to the Hanging in there, but then L would have had to explain
something perhaps painful to someone he did not know that well, I
concluded, concluding also that I had probably done the right thing,
inadequate though it may have been. For we were not friends, L & I.
In fact, I always have to remind myself of his name—L, as opposed to
R. I considered these matters on the drive home, the sky a high bright
blue, the breezes jostling a few palm leaves and making them shine.
When I slowed at a stop sign, there came a noise of birds so strident
and clamorous and terrifyingly close that I had to check my backseat to
make sure they had not gotten into the car.

THE MIGRATING WALL

There was a wall of Ruth and Sam's house that bordered the neighbor's bed of ivy. These neighbors allowed the ivy to spread unchecked. It crawled up the wooden fence and weighed it down so that the fence now listed dangerously to one side. Then it overtook Ruth's carefully tilled flowerbeds and strangled the roses. It even made its way toward their house after dark, sneaking up like a band of terrorists. For a while, she'd tried to tear it out, whacking at it with shears, brutalizing tendrils and shredding the sharp little leaves, but it continued to spread and grow like a cancer, she told Sam, just like a bad cancer, a melanoma.

The neighbors were oblivious. He was the sort of man who was addicted to Internet porn and she was an hysteric with a loud voice. When she wasn't gossiping, she was listening to the conversations of others. Neither had time to attend to the unruly ivy.

We could try poison, Sam told Ruth. There's a kind of poison that will kill ivy, I'm pretty sure. But we wouldn't want it to kill the cat, said Ruth. True, said Sam.

They were getting ready to go to bed. Ruth had smeared on some kind of cream which caused her face to gleam in an unpleasant way. Why she always got so greased up before bed was a mystery to Sam, who was propped up on the pillows reading a magazine article about one of the candidates. Perhaps it was a way of avoiding sex. Hey get this, he said, and he went on to read a very long and tangled criticism of that candidate's economic policies.

I wish this election were over, Ruth said, so you could talk about something else. I am passionately concerned, he agreed. Then they turned out the light.

The next morning the neighbor's ivy was gone and in its place was another part of the city. How odd, said Ruth, regarding a group of children with spray cans of paint and another group of children passing envelopes to people in cars in return for cash. We seem to have changed neighborhoods overnight. She stood at the window that had formerly held a view of the brick sides of the neighbors' house and all that ivy. Sam was in the kitchen grinding the beans for their coffee. Usually the noise of the grinder overpowered every other noise, but this morning it was very faint in the din coming from the city street: cars honking, tires screeching, sirens, glass breaking, gun shots, et cetera.

When she joined Sam in the kitchen, things were calmer. The view from that window was the same as always—a bland lawn (theirs) and a tree with a twisted trunk, like the arms of a contortionist. Something's happened, Ruth said, and she explained. Sam rolled his eyes. You are a dreamer Ruth, a big funny dreamer. Come look for yourself, said Ruth. In a minute, said Sam. First I'm going to drink my coffee and then check my email. Maybe there's some new news.

Ruth returned to the bedroom. She considered it possible that she'd invented this strange turn of events, as wish fulfillment. Perhaps her desire to banish the neighbor's ivy extended to the neighbors themselves—it was entirely possible. She disliked them. Once the woman told her that she overheard "every word" of Ruth's telephone conversations. So you should keep your voice down, concluded the woman triumphantly. Another time, the man offered her a very strong gin and tonic when Sam was at work. Stupidly, she drank it and became drunk and wound up laughing with the man over nothing. After that, he'd acted as though they had a special bond.

Yes, her mind might have been playing tricks on her. But when she went to their bedroom window she saw a group of police with clubs chasing the kids with the spray cans of paint and one of the kids shot a spray of silver paint on their bedroom window as she raced passed. This was a lanky, awkward-looking girl wearing a baseball cap and very orange lipstick. For a moment, Ruth thought she would come crashing into the bedroom.

Sam! Ruth shouted, but when Sam didn't answer she thought the better of it. Why involve Sam? He would find out sooner or later and it would make him angry. He would blame her. He would think that her obsession with the ivy had produced this consequence. That's the way Sam was. He was a fan of the status quo—and Ruth, he believed, always threatened to tamper with it.

He sat in front of his laptop, finger-mousing his way through the New York Times. He was obsessed with the upcoming election because it meant, he explained to Ruth, a new chapter in history. Our hopes and dreams will be fulfilled, he prophesied, sounding a little too much like a sound bite from his candidate's stump speech.

But really, there was nothing more important these days, he thought, pausing at the latest Gallup, which favored a landslide. Outside the birds were chirping, a sound most pleasant on this Sunday morning and Ruth, mercifully, had ceased to call out to him. He imagined her industriously cleaning out a drawer or sewing a button, though these were things Ruth never did. In the distance, he thought he heard her cry out and what that was about he did not know. Ruth was not the type of person given to crying out.

Not for the first time, Sam considered his choice of Ruth. That he could have done better occurred to him occasionally; everyone had told him so way back when. His ex-wife had been especially adamant. She is not your type, mark my words, Myranda had said. But, at the time, Sam could not be deterred. Ruth's sensibility appealed to him—he had seen her as eccentric and cultivated. Now he believed her neurotic.

What's so funny? he shouted, because suddenly he heard her whoop with laughter. Nothing! Ruth shouted back and then broke into a fresh bout of laughter. He knew from the sound of it that whatever it was would not amuse him. He would rather be checking the news on his candidate anyway.

The thing about the candidate was that he heard from him everyday. A personalized email that began, "Dear Sam," and then went on to report the progress of the election. Sam knew that the email was not really from the candidate, but he still liked the idea of getting this correspondence: to pretend that the actual candidate had emailed him, that he and the candidate had a personal relationship was only a small leap of faith under the circumstances. He liked to imagine the candidate calling him up for advice or just to relax and laugh on the phone, the candidate confiding, "if it weren't for you—" and "man, I really need your help." In fact, the emails themselves said something similar to the above, which is why Sam found himself donating more and more money to the candidate's campaign.

Ruth did not know why she was laughing, but on she laughed. She beheld a city under a hot, flat sky: the homeless and their shopping carts piled with bottles and rags; dead-eyed teenagers plugged into headphones; taxis screeching to curbs to retrieve or deposit business-suited passengers with hard mouths. Across the street, a tall building had sprung up, gunmetal grey with row upon row of window squares that put Ruth in mind of hundreds of blind eyes, staring down at her.

Ruth no longer cared if Sam joined her at the window. It seemed to her that it was all a joke, the house, the ivy, the incomprehensible city street—even Sam himself, her partner in another room, was a form of tragic irony perpetuated by the gods, whoever the gods were. She laughed a little bitterly.

And Sam called from the other room. What's so goddamned funny? But she didn't answer. She didn't want to hear his voice.

Gripping the sill, she stuck her head out. A hot breeze slapped the sides of her neck, the sun dug into her hair. A mother dragged a child by one arm; a cat huddled near a fire escape. Three women brushed by, so close she could smell their perfume. Arm in arm, they walked, speaking in high, beautiful voices. Right where the ivy had been so recently flourishing, a pigeon with an iridescent throat flapped its wings.

What to make of any of this, Ruth did not know. It was like a certain kind of dream, unbearably sad and unbearably real.

Sam listened to Ruth's laughter fade, the way you might suddenly realize that a movie or dream were about to end or that one phase of your life were about to vanish forever. He felt the urge to touch her, to enfold her in his arms, to preserve a little last shred of her laughter, to feel it tremble against his chest.

HOMELESS CAT

Into our lives comes a small cat, scratching at the screen door, its expression weary and disillusioned. Oh come in, we say, and we give it a little saucer of milk, which it laps up. Then it begins to talk to us in our own language. It is full of complaints concerning the economy, the world energy situation and life on this planet, the great mystery being that we weren't consulted, we are helpless pawns of the universe, yadda yadda. In other words, not only a smart cat, but a phenomenally bitter cat.

WHEREWITHAL

Today my old friend Raymond was pushing a shopping cart down
Speedway, the shopping cart overflowing with clothes, Raymond
unshaven and very dirty. Did you see that? I said. Raymond must have
fallen on hard times. Not at all, said my companion. It is well known
that Raymond is leading a double life. He is not content merely with
a life of property, my companion went on. He feels that his half-time
homelessness puts everything into perspective. I gave it some thought.
Of all my friends, Raymond is the laziest; therefore, he would be the last
person I'd expect to muster up the wherewithal to pull off a stunt like
this.

TOY DOG

A man with a toy dog on a leash stood on line in front of me. This item was tan with round glass eyes. It jerked to the right and left, mimicking to a T a dog's impatience. A little fringe of white acrylic fur made a stiff canopy over each eye, but its lips were black and twitching like the lips of an actual dog. The man bent over and whispered something to the dog at which point the dog collapsed on the floor, rested its chin on the carpeting and gazed up at me. At me! What amazing workmanship! I thought to myself, and for a moment I had an urge to stroke it or feed it a treat.

BARK

The dog is barking again and the family is annoyed. The barking dog represents a glitch in their system; they suspect the dog expresses the family's secret malaise. For this reason they decide to feed the dog poisonous meat.

There is something existential about the dog's bark. It is not as if it hopes to gain anything like a nice biscuit or even the negative attention of a swift kick; it is more that the woof-woofing spirals up from its wrenched soul, a rant against things of the world, both pleasant and unpleasant—the McDonald's dumpster as well as a swarm of yellow jackets stinging its neck, it's all the same to the dog.

The dog is black with a small pond of tan in the middle of its back. Its ears: twin beige trees. Its nose a circle of mud.

Dad: a hard-faced man with a big belly sits at the end of the sofa and reads the want ads. When he finds one of interest he encircles it in blue ball point and reads it aloud to the family.

Radio announcer/Pr Hack wanted to disparage enemies of regime.
Ex college prof required for re-education of 90 yr old millionaire with cats.

The ads make no sense to anyone in the family. What do they mean *regime*? asks the daughter. Whose regime? It sounds fishy to me.

Everything sounds fishy to you, says Mom. There are times, Gwen, when you have to take a little on faith. Otherwise you'll wind up a recluse with no friends and no worldly connections. You'll dwell in a cave with no money and an incurable disease. Just you wait and see, young lady!

On the other hand, it makes no sense to Mom that cats are included in the millionaire reeducation ad. Why cats? What could cats possibly have to do with anything? she wonders.

Remember this, says Darryl, wisely, we don't always have to know everything. There are some things beyond our knowledge and even to speculate about them would be to drive ourselves a little nuts.

This is what I was saying, son, says Mom. I was saying exactly the same thing.

No, says Darryl, you employed the word "faith" and I am a pragmatist who is simply acknowledging the limitations of the human mind.

I will take my chances and apply for both jobs, says Dad. Even though I have no idea what is called for in either.

Why should you know? asks Mom. You don't need to know everything.

You *can't* know everything, amends Darryl.

Just then the doorbell rings and into the room comes Bing who is Gwen's date for the evening. Hi ho, says Bing, who is wearing some kind of executioner outfit: a tight-fitting black mask and some studded paraphernalia including gloves which he removes in order to shake Dad's hand.

Dude, you're such a freak, says Darryl, disdaining the hand of Bing. Why are you such a freak? He says this to the world at large, as if the world at large were gazing in at this family scene which is, in fact, Darryl's fantasy. In his happiest times he believes his life is being televised and he tries to conduct himself accordingly.

Just then the dog commences to bark again. Woof woof woof woof.

Sooner or later someone has to see to the dog, says Mom. I thought you'd take care of that Dad. Some of us are gainfully employed and we count on those others to pick up the slack. You could at least poison the dog.

I said I'd take care of it and I will, says Dad.

Mom is not gainfully employed but she is fucking the neighbor which takes up a good deal of her time. On top of that, she cooks dinner, does laundry, carpools, and so on.

There's no need to car pool any more, says Gwen. We're grown up.

Give up the carpool, says Darryl. It's a completely useless activity. If you gave up the carpool you'd have time to poison the dog.

Why don't you poison the dog, it was your idea, says Gwen to Darryl.

I really *am* gainfully employed, says Darryl. I support this family with my drug dealing.

Darryl sells a new designer drug that makes everyone believe their lives are being televised. People who take this drug go around in states of euphoria born of fleeting self-importance. Darryl himself is addicted to this drug which is called PLAY which is an acronym for Please Look At Yourself.

How about a cocktail? Mom asks Bing. I could use a cocktail, says Bing, I've had a hard day in the fields. What fields may those be? asks Gwen. It's just an expression, says Bing. I doubt that, says Gwen. Oh, give him a break, says Darryl. Let the poor guy enjoy his cocktail. The mom has just handed Bing a cocktail made of rum and tomato juice called a RAT which is an acronym for Rum And Tomato.

The dad has found an ad that is in search of a telemarketer with a lisp.

132

Listhen to thith, says the dad, Lithping telemarketer needed for thales and showth.

What kind of shows? asks the mom. It doethn't thay, says the dad. It's just plain screwy, says Gwen. Perhaps you'll be required to wear a dress, too.

I'm not a thithy! I'm not a thithy! says Dad, enjoying himself.

Perhaps a lisping sales person puts people at ease, suggests the mom. True. People feel superior to those with disabilities, says Darryl. I'm not dithabled! I'm not dithabled! shouts Dad.

Just then Bing vomits on the couch. His vomit is red with little specks of pink and yellow—little pieces of what look like salami and some cheddar cheese, possibly. The mask he wears is stained red around the mouth-hole which makes him look as if he'd devoured a live mammal.

Now that's a turn on, says Gwen sarcastically. Don't worry about it, says Darryl, clapping Bing on the back, you aren't the first. I'm so sorry, says Mom. It may have been the cocktail.

We hope it's the cocktail! says Darryl. That is its purpose.

Just then Charlie enters the living room with his wife Wendy who is on a leash today. It's very comfortable, she reports. You would think the tugging at the neck would cause irritation but I find it oddly relaxing to be tugged and led. Sometimes you lead, says Charlie affectionately. True, I do lead sometimes. And I get to poop on the sidewalk.

Just then the real dog barks hoarsely—ruff ruff ruff ruff ruff—as if weary of its own angst and the barking that accompanies it. If only I were happy, thinks the dog, who cannot conceive of happy as more than a rhyme for "snappy" or "flappy" or as an acronym for He Accumulates Pathetic Pitiful Years.

The sooner that dog is out of the way, the better, says Dad. Maybe we should draw straws, says Gwen. Especially since we have guests—it increases the odds. True. Maybe a guest will draw the short straw, says the mom. Maybe *Charlie* will draw the short straw, says the mom winking at Charlie.

Charlie is the neighbor man the mom is servicing in her free time. He needs more sex than I can give him, says Wendy about this arrangement. I'm actually grateful to the mom for being so generous with her time and energy. In fact, that's why we're here. To express our gratitude, interjects Charlie. We have a nice plaque, adds Wendy. Where is it Charlie? After all this did you leave it at home? I can't believe I'm so stupid, says Charlie. I'm such an idiot.

What a coincidence! says Dad, who has just then found an ad for idiots which reads *Idiots wanted for medical study, must have IQ under 60 &/or pathologically impaired judgment.*

That's you in a nutshell, says Mom. I guess I could feign stupidity, says Dad. It pays surprisingly well. I'm glad that's settled, says Darryl who is preening for an imaginary camera. It's good to have an employed Dad. It's the American way and god knows we love America and her way (WLAAHW). He smiles charmingly.

Do we love her curds or just her whey? quips Mom. Speaking of turds, Bing throws up again, but it is clear liquid vomit, the dry heaves, nearly curdless. I really feel like shit, he announces rudely.

Time to rip off the mask! cries Gwen. Give it here! She begins tearing a little corner of the mask near Bing's neck. You don't want to do that, says Bing. There's no telling what you'll find beneath. True, it might be something really horrible like a no-nosed monster, says Mom. Or it could be a person without skin, says Darryl. We would all faint and Bing would steal our computers. You're right, says Gwen, it isn't worth it. Truth be told, I'm not even that curious.

Are we going to draw those straws or not? asks Dad. Because the dog is barking again and this time it is a brisk *yip yip yip yip* that assaults the family's ears. Nothing worse than a yipper, says Mom. I'll get the straws.

Here's an ad for straws; it says *Wanted, straws for underprivileged crippled children.* We don't have extras, says Darryl. They should really find their own straws, says Gwen. It's not as if they're completely helpless.

Why would they want straws anyway? asks the mom. It doesn't make sense. We could sell them straws, says the dad, so I wouldn't have to work.

Just then Wendy gets her leash mixed up in Charlie's pant legs and she bites him angrily. Just then the mom pops a PLAY pill and imagines she is an Iron Chef competitor making braised eel. Just then the dad finds an ad for braised eel look-a-likes. Just then Darryl thinks it would be good TV if he whipped out his own eel-look-a-like and brandished it at the camera. Just then Bing throws up again. And finally someone— Gwen!—feeds poisonous meat to the barking dog.

Arf arf arf arf arf, says the dog who has not yet begun to die. Momentarily the landscape will be draped in shadow, the hills swathed and hushed, the dog dying and barking, barking and dying.

THE CORPSE AND ITS ADMIRERS

The coffin is grey with gold curlicues at the corners, at each of the four corners, although we only see two from where we are sitting with our mother. Each curlicue of a golden color has a shiny ring of silver around it and then some dots. The dots are very small.

The oak casket is very big. It is 10 feet. Maybe it is 20 feet. The feet of the corpse jut up from it since it is a shallow casket. Picture a pork chop in a crepe pan and that is how the body looks in the casket: jutting up, the nose pointed and white, the feet in their brown cordovans.

Our mother is crying. She is fishing around in her patent leather purse while crying and her face is very red and ugly. Picture a wadded-up piece of cloth soaked in bloody nose damage and you will get the feeling of her face. In her patent leather purse are the following items: sunglasses, a movie ticket stub from *The Paradine Case* starring Gregory Peck who falls in love with an imprisoned woman, Kleenex, Lifesavers, both of which are in blue and white packages.

For a murderess, the Paradine woman is exceptionally well-dressed.

The purse of our mother has a gold clasp shaped like a fish.

Also there is some change at the bottom and some flakes of tobacco, given that our mother is trying to quit smoking cigarettes.

We are embarrassed at the noises our mother makes when she weeps. Picture a siren interrupted by a braying sheep and also a coughing giant and you will have some idea how she sounds.

I myself am sewing a sleeve on a blouse.

The corpse does nothing. This is its advantage. There is a fly on the casket, resting languidly on one of the blond oak lintels. In a bad mood.

Now, my sister whispers, *he* will have no more bad moods.

I myself nod wisely, the blouse which is of a silky and thus slippery material slithers around on my little lap.

Yes, I say. I have only 10 stitches to go. Maybe 20. Then I will sew a little something onto my sister's head who has begged me for some time to do this.

The corpse's nose is long and white-tipped. From here we can only imagine the soft flare of the nostrils. Or maybe it is a hard flare. We can vaguely recall the teeth, yellow from the smoking of Pall Malls.

My mother who has given up smoking now removes a black veil from her purse. 10 feet long. Or 20 feet. Very long, it unfolds and unfolds, it seems this unfolding will go on forever, my sister Razor whispers to me, and soon we are covered in it, like insects trapped in a spider's web.

My mother is bald and so is my sister. Once, at her request, I stitched the words WEIRD ZONE onto my mother's scalp.

My father, who is dead, is not a skinhead but a corpse.

My mother covers us with her veil, still weeping, still shuddering under the veil but now we are part of that shuddering since, beneath the spider web veil, my sister, my mother and I make one shape.

We are thus part of the shape of my mother.

My father is crying in his casket but his tears are the tears of corpses which go inward and keep the body from thawing and melting away.

The blouse is made of vinyl (I think) and has little rubber buttons. I am sewing the sleeve, I just realized, in the wrong place.

Inside the coffin my father is sneezing. My mother reaches into her purse. Once more she reaches into it and this time removes a half dozen tacos which she divides among us. Then salsa and little plates of rice. Then spoons.

My father, when alive, was not a sneezer. He was not an eater. He had his moods which hammered themselves into our tumbling home, into our mother's makeshift spirit. He was not a weeper.

No thank you, I tell our mother. Even so, I cannot seem to work up an appetite. The corpse is still sneezing and weeping, more copiously now: picture a jackhammer drilling into a human brain and you will have some idea of the racket which is beginning to assert itself into the air surrounding the coffin.

Perhaps he has allergies, my sister whispers.

All the while I am stitching the sleeve on the blouse—and it is going much, much better now, thanks for asking, creating a neat little seam in the shape of scythe. I am trying to think of a prayer to say for my father's soul and the effort to do so makes me recall several moments: jumping rope, my father at one end, laughing with his mouth full; or driving over the bridge, my father saying he was frightened and so could not look; or singing for him at a large party and his face beaming and beaming. Hard to believe a face so white and frozen could have beamed so warmly or that in the cave of his arm we had felt so protected. Nevertheless.

The Paradine woman, a master of duplicity, manages to destroy Gregory Peck whom she hates for luring her lover (Louis Jordan) into suicide. His career over, his love unrequited and disdained, he returns to his nice wife (Ann Todd) who comforts him like a mother.

Not that our own mother is all that comforting. She distributes tacos from her voluminous purse and now she is chewing loudly. So many noises in this room! My mother chewing and swallowing, my father weeping and sneezing, my sister whispering, and I am making the sound of she who stitches a sleeve onto a blouse and who will soon stitch a little something onto the scalp of my sister.

The great moral lesson of *The Paradine Case* is that we should not trust attractive foreigners, no matter how beautifully dressed. Another way of saying this is that we must stay within our familiar realm and not venture forth. Don't flirt with danger. Be safe. Or for me, a stitch in time saves nine.

Now that the father is dead, our lives will surely change. He who had been our armor, our jailer. He who stabbed us with his words and then caressed us. We who were stabbed, then caressed, defended and incarcerated. We may have murdered him, too.

At some point it occurs to me that we are all everything, that nothing separates us. Picture a parade of ants going toward a picnic arranged on a red-and-white-checked tablecloth and then picture a foot coming down. We are all things. The ants, the picnic and the foot.

THE NEW NEW MUSIC

Lim Kim & her band of sister-wives by the screen door. Close-up of
Lim Kim's eyeball. Ferret spike. Guitar strum. Hash of dust overhead
where hats had once graced the metropolis. Debris includes a corset,
macerated eraser, anthill, sketchbook. Doe-colored plastic bags open &
fill not unlike an eye scanning the arena, becoming bored, shutting.

Pencil tucked in hairnet, Benny gangling in, heart-height, ready for a
jot. The green hammock sways in its space of green. Lim Kim taps her
bare foot. The sister-wives in unison say We are the propagators, the
progenitors, the sister-wives, the dozens of us like one thing, oh oh oh.

Benny poised for a note-take, the new new music swell on the porch,
the screen door clap-flap, the sister-wives haircuts severe & stationary.

Yearning is a thing of the past, Lim Kim announces. We are no longer
cool with it. Bye bye blues. & goodbye to burnt coffee & dat man who
don't come home. Goodbye to all dat gloomy weather wherein da phone
don't ring & da mail don't come.

Benny has a whippet on a chain, balloons sizzling from its neck-ring.
Lim Kim these days missing a tooth, whistles meatily: a grander, hipper
sound than previous, Benny has to admit.

~

In another part of the metropolis Muscle Man Cole with a snowy chest
parades the seashore, black socks to mid-calf.

But even the sea has moved on to contemporary pitches & moans.
Almost impossible to discern among the wheeling gulls, the dust-clouds

whose narratives drift into sub-topics & estuaries.

Lagoon on her way somewhere, black-hatted, sunglasses with pearled rosettes large satchel of plastic weave into which she lobs seashells, feathers, clumps of sea grass hard as toenails.

Birds open their pie holes, lurp into the sea. Muscle Man a hesitation at the sea's edge ripples his furrow. Birds are so cool, he proclaims loud enough for an osprey to blink awake, screech through a dust castle & caw-caw.

Not a pretty sight, Lagoon says to Sally, brand new Sally. Having recently joined the narrative, Sally has no progenitors. I agree, though, nods to Lagoon. Of Muscle Man Cole who has begun to scratch his behind. What gets into people? Sally wonders. Out in public view amongst the public?

~

At the casa of sister-wives, even an egg scramble takes on a duh-duh in the face of the new news. Lim Kim at the forefront. Brandishing a spatula as if to instruct the others to partake. It's a time to be more like ants, she argues, super-organizing so that we won't. Won't what? says Benny who beautifully moans between phrases. The whippet as well.

We wonder, then, summarily, if it's just a little bit over-designed, self-annihilating, its structuralism touting Barthes in a cowardly *nostalgie*. Not that either, says Lim Kim. She know what she want. She know what she invent for da purpose. The new new music, as opposed to the old new music, where one guy played a little, then another become King. Where the sister-wives braided each others' hair to the beat of the tom tom tom.

Any minute Lagoon, Sally arrive, Muscle Man Cole in tow, osprey scent faint upon clothing. It's all pheromones all the time from now on. Even while the universe darkens, especially so in the dark, creepy caves of this our earth, its intermittency, its big noise.

THE STORY OF MS BARBARA HOWE

Ms Barbara Howe, walking on the beach near her home in Santa
Monica, where she lived with her brother Frederick and her dog Curl,
so named for his tail, discovered a rare shell on her morning walk. At
first—she reported—she thought it was a shoe.

Ms Barbara Howe possessed a lovely singing voice and used to sing
in her church choir. After a while the climb up to the church balcony
where the choir and organ were lodged became too much for her and
so she resigned. The teenagers in the choir were not sorry to see her go.
Despite her fine voice, she exuded an air of disapproval and they could
not help but feel she was judging them for the very things they could
not help: their young bodies and minds.

Ms Barbara Howe, as a child, had been outgoing and sunny. A popular
teenager, she later married a man with a job at a bank. She'd always kept
her hair pulled back to show off her ears which her mother told her were
her finest feature. An ear is like a shell with its graceful design of whorls
and spirals leading, like a fugue played on a cello, to a dark, mysterious
interior.

Ms Barbara Howe moved in with her brother Frederick after her
husband left her for one of the bank tellers, a glamorous woman older
than he by five years, what they call "a cougar" these days. Frederick was
younger than Barbara by five years and Barbara had been younger than
her husband by three years.

Ms Barbara Howe was fond of saying Life Throws You Curves.
Sometimes, before she resigned from the choir, Barbara enjoyed
throwing in some fanciful trills to spark up songs that were otherwise a
little too solemn for her taste. When she was met with resistance from

the choir master, a traditionalist with a lisp and a meticulously groomed moustache parked on his upper lip, she complained that too little innovation in church music might lead to a repressive, cold religious practice. Music can make everything new, she was also fond of saying.

The seashell Ms Barbara Howe discovered, shaped like a shoe, and still harboring a little creature within its deep vortices, was green. Now that's unusual, her friend remarked. A green sea shell. Perhaps it isn't a sea shell at all, said Barbara.

When she first moved in with her brother Frederick, she was greeted with exceedingly disarrayed premises. Frederick, a cheerful, silent fellow, hadn't washed a dish in months; he'd allowed the dishes, plus pots and pans, to pile up on any surface not yet occupied by unopened mail, laundry, and the various knickknacks that had belonged to their mother and now had been pushed nonchalantly to one side to make room for everything else. Although he had a perfectly good job as a manager of a retail store, he spent his hours away from work holed up in his room watching pornography. Unashamed of his unusual hobby, he claimed that it relaxed him to watch the sexual interactions of others. When he left the house, Frederick wore suits and the thin ties that had belonged to their father.

Living near the beach was a lucky thing, always there were cool breezes and a good smell of salt. Nostalgia is sensual and Ms Barbara Howe surrendered to it in the same way she'd surrendered to her future husband on their first date, his lovely smell, his clean-shaven neck.

Her friend wore a camel's hair jacket and a woolen cap. Barbara wore blue jeans, a red sweater and a checked scarf. For some time they passed the shell between them. There seemed to be a small noise issuing from its interior, but each was afraid to listen closely.

About Curl the dog: he was not afraid of many things. The world, such as it was, struck him as small and endurable. He was fond of Ms Barbara

Howe, his benefactor or his slave, depending on one's point of view, but was not given to affectionate gestures, per se. He enjoyed running and napping. His curiosity was not voluminous but reasonable. He was not inclined to nudge his canine nose into the odd shell any more than the women in his company were. Not afraid so much as prudent.

Ms Barbara Howe had never needed to work since her husband, the banker, wracked with guilt over having left her for an older woman— supplied her with alimony. Frederick, likewise, took care of the household expenses. Though his pornography habit or hobby ran him into the hundreds per month, he made a good salary at the store, a large renowned chain store wherein almost anything one needed for life could be purchased.

In any case, Ms Barbara Howe was not a shopper. She enjoyed her friend, in whom she confided, and she enjoyed collecting shells. This shell, however, gave her pause.

The friend removed her woolen cap, turned it inside out and dropped the shell inside. The sun had long since disappeared behind a cloud, it had been there for weeks, hiding out glumly, and the sky was all one color, a color that was hard to name. Curl, the noble dog, if I may say so, was running out of earshot so that when Ms Barbara Howe called to him, as he knew she would sooner or later, he had the handy excuse of not having heard. It was his deepest wish to escape Ms Barbara Howe and go live in a cave with gypsies, but gypsies were not around these parts, as far as he could tell.

Like most who are addicted to pornography, Frederick had vexed relationships with the objects of his sexual fantasies. Women made him awkward and shy in real life. Ms Barbara Howe informed him he had issues with intimacy and occasionally it worried him to think this might be so. Other than that, he was a happy guy who worked hard to keep the shelves properly stocked even though he was rarely the one to do the heavy lifting. The other employees respected him because he was fair and because he was quiet. It is interesting that quiet people earn more respect than their chatty counterparts.

The building that housed the chain retail store that Frederick managed was square and grey, and duplicated many such buildings that housed many such stores in this famous chain of stores. Typically this store would move into a community, buy a large lot and eventually slap up their signature square grey behemoth and before you knew it the local stores were priced out of business. This is capitalism, explained Frederick to his sister, and she concurred, though she did not approve.

What if, said her friend in the camel's hair coat, the creature inside this shell were from another world? You mean an ET? said Ms Barbara Howe. Something like that, said the friend. There is definitely something spooky about this shell, agreed Ms Barbara Howe. I know, it felt as if it were burning my hand, said the friend, which is why I had to get rid of it. They both surveyed the shell at the bottom of the woolen hat and beneath the slashing sounds of sea breezes they could have sworn they heard something.

To Barbara the sound resembled a song she used to sing in the choir, a hymn to Christ Almighty invoking angels and worship and death. But her friend heard something entirely different, not so melodic, the noise of freeway traffic or an egg white being whipped into a froth. Christ is risen Christ will rise again, Ms Barbara Howe remembers.

And so you see, Ms Barbara Howe's story is not eventful. Do not expect events. If you keep reading, you will encounter more of the same: Curl the dog, disgruntled that his companions seem to have forgotten about him, wandering slowly home, humiliated. Frederick, a willing pawn of the state or the store or the culture, climbing for once a ladder, then dismounting, then realizing that a mosquito has stabbed him on the wrist, then enjoying a bright evening of pornography. Ms Barbara Howe parting ways with her friend at the corner flanked by stately palm trees. Twilight through the fronds. Curl safely in tow woof-woofing. Beautiful details like the grey swirl at the outermost edge of the shell's languid orbit. A noise faint and fainter. A sudden elevation of Ms Barbara Howe's mood replaced by its opposite.

Listen: The drone of a plane.

Everything else miles into the future.

THE SNOW QUEEN

Prologue

In the mirror her face was deeply unfamiliar, the mouth drawn down at the corners, the eyes blank, strange, lacking expression, as if over the real face someone had substituted a mask with an image of another face. Whose?

Always this question: who are you? Now the face, the one that is not her own, is aging, the jaw line has become wobbly and the neck has developed heavy folds pulling what was once a solemn long face down even further, almost a parody of the face that once was. A melted face, less distinct than before, on the verge of disappearing. Not hers.

I took a course in psychoanalytic theory and Jacques Lacan was the star of that course. One felt, reading Lacan, that he was always the star of any course in which he happened to reside. It was Lacan who pronounced the mirror-image a *misprision*—a misperception.

I thought knowing these things would help me understand. But what I discovered is that what I hadn't understood became even more complicated: a simple box with a secret inside had grown limbs and appendages each with more secrets and little branches attached to the limbs and appendages, and dots on the branches that vibrated with whatever it was they hid. It was as if all knowledge were inaccessible, constantly galloping ahead or lagging behind or on another planet. In such a way, the world was restored to mystery and I took a certain pleasure in knowing that I couldn't know anything.

It wasn't that Lacan was so difficult (though he was difficult). Many understood him perfectly and had a good time arguing about the implications of his theories. For me, though, it was as if I had glimpsed a little puddle at the bottom of a well—very far away and menacing though the menace may just have been the distance of the puddle from the edge of the well over which I peered and which I might have imagined falling into. . . . The puddle also held my image, very dark and quivering and tiny, my face looking down in a manner almost sublime. Though it wasn't my face. I may have been frightened.

Lacan's Mirror Stage refers to the time at which a child first perceives himself in the mirror—*Voilà !* But the self he sees is a fantasy of a self which can never be known.

Is it possible I skipped this crucial step in my own evolution? (Was she right not to recognize her own image, her mistaken image that, to her, always felt alien?)

Like the mirror, the mother's body is shattered and the child does not see this at first, thinking she is whole and ideal. Thinking she is he and he is she. In the mirror which is broken but appears unbroken.

Still there is this: A child whom the mother loves. A mother whom the child loves. Together they are disturbingly one.

I remember waking up with my son in my arms. He must have been about ten minutes old. His head was horribly lopsided and he had purple marks on his temples where they used the forceps. Naturally I began to weep uncontrollably. On the other side of the plate glass window in my hospital room, I watched a flock of birds zoom by; they seemed to be cackling. One came quite close to the window, even peered in at us, my son and I in the high, white hospital bed, him swaddled in a blue and white striped flannel blanket and me in a pink bed jacket trimmed with lace over a black bra. It peered in at us and it was then that I noticed that it wasn't a bird at all, but a tiny demon with horns made out of icicles.

1

I'd just moved back to the city and it was snowing, but it always seemed to be snowing here those days, even when it wasn't snowing one had the impression of snow. I'd moved back to the city, having been away for a long time, and so my return felt unreal, as if I were sitting in a calm chair by a fire and straining (and failing) to recall a home I'd left so long ago—I cannot even say how long ago, in fact, because upon returning everything blurred, especially time blurred, becoming fuzzy around the edges like an old mitten.

I'd been away for a long time during which I'd produced quite a bit of work. I'd been industrious, this at least you can say about me. And though I am no judge of this work, I can say in all honesty that I'd given it my all: all my strength and life's blood; as they say, I'd poured my heart into it. You might liken my project to architecture, to plans for building a vision out of innovative materials, a kind of esoteric blueprint for what I conceived of for, say, an expression of life. I'd become very absorbed to the point of ignoring the world spinning and dipping around me . . . I came back hoping to connect, to find myself again. I believe we are always losing and finding ourselves.

After two weeks of wandering around, I ran into a friend at Borders bookstore who very generously offered me a place to stay at his apartment. I suppose it was pity when my friend asked where I was living or if I had a place to stay for the night. My general look of forlornness must have prompted him to say, I happen to have a free sofa, and he winked at me, which I considered very kind, very warm-hearted of this friend who, as I recall, did not have a reputation for either warmth or kindness.

We were browsing the psychology section, he holding a book on the borderline personality and I holding a similar volume concerning narcissism. The *maladies du jour*, quipped my friend, if you don't count drug addiction. Ah yes, drug addiction, I said vaguely. I wasn't sure I wanted to discuss drug addiction with this friend. I had known many drug addicts and they all were unbearably sad and I found it hard to be irreverent about them. One such was my own son, a pathetic person who wandered these city streets homeless, perpetually checking himself into and out of detox units and trying to scam me into purchasing phony prescriptions. I wanted to forget about my son, to excise him from my mind, but the more I tried to do this, the more his presence asserted itself and I could see him, as if a movie were flickering before my eyes, as a serious, overalled toddler and then as a tender, pudgy pre-teen with straight brown hair that hung over one eye.

I did not want to discuss my son.

We are always finding and losing ourselves, it is the nature of our lives on earth.

My friend and I then repaired to the fiction section and explored the A's, Jane Austen, all the Andersons, Agee, Alcott and others, the usual great variety under A, and we each perused according to our tastes, slipping a book from the shelf, riffling through the pages and replacing it, but not before chuckling over a title or author photo, the way you do, but still in a state of awe—because books, written by anyone, are an achievement, even if they are not always ennobling.

I hadn't slept for a week. I'd been away and when I returned to this city I found everything changed. For example, a certain street I'd remembered as going one way toward the state capital now pointed in a different direction. Where this boulevard had been tree-lined, it was now flanked with tall soulless buildings. A store that used to sell small appliances had sprung up in the place of the junior college where I'd once taught freshman composition and all the cars had new-style garish license plates. I do not remember the state motto being _____, but it's possible I'd never really attended to the state motto. It was very cold, as I've said, snowing or about to—whereas before it had been temperate, tending toward sea breezes, balmy and blue. Now, no sea in sight (though I searched until I exhausted myself) and a strange odor permeated the air, a cold odor, not quite fresh, as of old snow, but so recent that it did not qualify as memory, but more like the fleeting space between nostalgia and dread, frozen into permanence.

My friend was blind in one eye, and though he assured me he'd always been blind in one eye—the result of a sleigh-riding accident when he was ten—I don't remember him being blind in one eye. You must have hidden it well, I remarked. At this, he bristled. It's not something you can exactly hide, he retorted. He was holding a paperback edition of H. C. Anderson's fairy tales—as far away from his face as his arms could stretch, since in addition to being blind in one eye he needed new reading glasses—and he insisted on sharing with me an excerpt from "The Snow Queen," which is all about a terrifying being called the Snow Queen who kidnaps a boy called Kay. I didn't want to be rude, but I'm not especially interested in fairy tales, no matter how capable and esteemed the author. In fact, "The Snow Queen" had a particularly perilous association for me, as she—the cold and beautiful woman—put me in mind of my mother who had once read me that story. Therefore, while my friend read—*it was a lady, tall and slender and brilliantly white. . .* —I let my mind wander.

2

For two weeks, I'd been looking for the sea, sleeping where I could under whatever canopy or ledge I could find—bridges, which had been abundant in the old days, had vanished without a trace, and so I was reduced to buttresses—the new gargoyles, snow-laden and hideous, the tiny balconies that used to be so fragrant and flower-laden, where people now smoked cigarettes, pitching the still-smoldering rockets below, almost burning me to death on several occasions.

I did not like to ask my friend—or anyone—about the sea since it is entirely possible that I am misremembering my old home. While he read

152

Anderson's "Snow Queen" in that excited way people have when they desperately want you to share their enthusiasm, their voices ratcheting up dramatically, my mind wandered the streets in the same manner as my body, for the past month, had wandered the streets. Still no sea.

My friend did not have the reputation for warmth or kindness, nevertheless he invited me to his apartment where he said there was an empty sofa with my name on it. He must have known I was extremely tired, yawning constantly and twirling and untwirling a strand of my hair around a forefinger, a habit when fatigued.

My friend said: All I ask is that you remember to put the shower curtain inside the tub. Otherwise the water will drip into the downstairs apartment and that bitch will have a fit. That's easy enough, I said. We hadn't even arrived at his apartment when he gave me this rule about the water and shower. I wondered if there were other rules that would be more difficult to follow because, like anyone, I worry about unconscious behaviors, those which I cannot control, and then I worry that I am too old to change.

I don't see well, said the friend apropos of nothing. We were walking down some avenue or other—I should say sliding down some avenue or other, since it had of course recently snowed and the road held the tracks of sleds and skis as well as snow tires and chains—but there was really nothing to see, I wanted to point out to my friend, everything was white, the sky, the street, and all the things that might have been visible on a day without snow were now covered with snow—rows of automobiles to the point that I wasn't sure they were automobiles. For all I knew, they might have been great hulking sea monsters who had lost the sea like the rest of us.

Nevertheless, I gave my friend my arm, and he clutched my red windbreaker which probably did the opposite of keeping me warm, it was of such a weird, cold material, and in this manner we eventually arrived at his apartment.

3

I was perfectly comfortable in my new surroundings; they beat the hell out of wandering the icy streets homeless, running into bands of thieves and drug addicts, my son not among those I'd encountered, thank god. I don't know what I would have done if I'd seen my pathetic son. My heart no longer bleeds for him, though there was a time when my heart was smashed to smithereens. Enough said. Every time I try to banish him from memory here he comes again with his tilted grey eyes, even in the guise of one whom I did not see in the past month, as he who had been conspicuously absent from my wanderings.

Being homeless is no picnic and, unlike my son, I did it drug free with only my thoughts for comfort, my belief (mistaken) that the sea lurked somewhere, waiting to restore me to my bearings.

My friend had a sofa, a TV, a lamp, a rug, a stove, a fridge, a double bed, a closet full of shoes and a cat. I hadn't realized he was such an austere fellow. He didn't have a reputation for warmth or kindness, but inviting me to his apartment suggested that this reputation was not entirely warranted.

I slept on the sofa, as instructed. It was foamy, not lumpy, and its velvet material a cocoon of sorts. We all like to feel swathed, I think. Also, my friend gave me a blanket—a nice blue blanket which I wrapped around myself multiple times—and a pillow that used to belong to the cat. In fact, the cat shared the pillow with me at night, which I didn't mind, the paddling and purring of the cat next to my ear as I slept, though I believe it colored my dreams.

The cat was cream-colored with large irregular splotches on its back, giving it the appearance of a small cow.

As cats go, it was medium-sized.

I dreamt of cows, therefore, and human infants who were pitched into dark holes and drug addicts sleeping on sofas belonging to other drug addicts.

The last time I saw my son he informed me that he was living in a "squat." I told him that that fact struck me as kind of ignominious.

I remember the ocean as being a deep gray color laden, on good days, with streaks of white, which gave it its characteristic shimmer. The sky on such days was lit with what looked to be rags hanging from a celestial clothesline. Very beautiful, but spooky.

4

My friend was christened Frederick von Schlegel, after the German philosopher of the same name, but everyone called him Hans. My name was G, just the initial deprived of the clothing, I liked to say. The cat's name was Fur and I won't tell you my son the drug addict's name.

I had been away for an indeterminate amount of time during which I completed a great deal of work. I kept residuals in a suitcase which, until I met Hans in Borders bookstore, I lugged around with me through the city. The bulk was housed elsewhere. I had no idea if any of it was successful. In more optimistic moments, I liked to think so; but eventually something would happen—the tiniest alteration in the atmosphere, such as the time when the crow who frequented the fire-escape railing growled at me through the window, and then I would be in despair over my accomplishments. At such times I felt I understood the impulses of those who scourged themselves with cat o' nine tails and slept on beds of nails. I, too, craved punishment for the unworthiness of my effort, indeed the unworthiness of my being.

Other than the sofa, Hans' apartment was replete with artificial flowers of every denomination. In the mornings, he would tend to these thousands with a translucent spray bottle, which would take a full hour. I could not shake the feeling that these flowers were about to speak, that there was more to them than twists of colored plastic or, in some cases, starched fabric. The cluster of pink ranunculus which sat stiffly on the coffee table in front of the sofa in which I slept seemed always about to discourse about psychology. The narcissist, they always seemed about to say, is generally a happier person than the comparatively hysterical borderline personality. Here they seemed to nod pointedly toward the daffodils, and I of course was reminded of my encounter with my friend at Borders bookstore when we each held those books on personality disorders only to abandon them (thankfully) for fiction. The tulips, I thought, seemed about to agree with me that the idea of personality disorders was kind of creepy and attractive at the same time, the notion that something surprising lurks under the surface of a person always a thrill, but perhaps, at times, an unwelcome thrill. On and on, the flowers seemed about to yak, and I admired their stamina. The fact that they all persisted in a season of profound winter was, I suppose, cause for celebration of some sort—or perhaps they were merely stir crazy, like me.

Even so, I rarely left the apartment, but settled myself by the window where I indulged in an on-and-off sprightly communication with the crow. The crow would bring me news of my son, not welcome news, and much as I tried to dissuade him (or her) from these reports, she seemed to insist upon delivering them. You never know about the sensibilities of other species who are possibly impervious to that which we hold dear as humans. In this case, I was holding dear the absence of my son from my life. I cherished this absence as some might cherish inhabiting the premises of one who collected artificial flowers of every denomination and harbored a spotted cat.

The cat was not a communicator and, aside from our sleep time, kept its distance. There were times when I felt it was "giving me a look," but many feel this way about cats on account of the shapes of their eyes and the fact that they rarely blink. Perhaps, though, they

have the capacity to stare into the soul; if this one had been able to
gaze into mine, I doubt it would have insisted on sleeping with me.
It would have discovered a clotted mess of conflicting desires and
repugnancies, all of which I hid behind my usual *sangfroid*.

Hans and I spoke rarely and when we did our conversation tended
to get caught up in snarls of misunderstanding. He was, as I've said,
blind in one eye, and this was the central fact of his life, to hear him
talk about it. Once I tried to tell him that being blind in one eye was
not all that disabling and he nearly bit my head off. You have no idea,
do you? he said incredulously, and we went on from there, back and
forth, like a ping pong tournament I remember participating in (and
losing) as a ten-year-old. Nerve-wracking to see that little white ball—
innocuous as it may have been—barreling toward you, as if it might
cripple you for life, which is the spirit in which we fought, Hans and I.
You are the most self-indulgent person I've ever met, he shouted and
I shouted, At least I'm not deluded and he shouted, You could at least
tidy up a little around here and I shouted, I can't hear myself think
around here!

This last was a mean-spirited reference to Hans' incessant theremin
playing, the spooky sounds reminiscent of bad sci fi or a copulating
cat or, less frequently, a flock of warbling mourning doves. Hans had
not yet mastered the instrument which was a difficult instrument to
master, though if you asked me anyone with a decent soprano could
mime the sounds pretty accurately by intoning ooooo and eeeee to the
tune of something plaintive.

When he played *O Mi Bambino Cara*, though, in spite of myself, I was
moved. There he would stand, at the helm of his peculiar instrument,
a lumpen figure of a man with a large square head, his mouth pressed
in a grim line, his hands like big roast beefs paddling the air—and
the tender spectacle of this sad, blind-in-one-eye man, along with
the Puccini—all the more poignant for being a little off-key—would
unfailingly bring tears to my eyes.

I was settling in like a cat settles in, surrendering myself to unfamiliar surroundings, marking my own tiny territory, as it were, which consisted of the sofa and a plastic chair I had moved to the window for the purpose of looking outside. It was always snowing or about to snow and it fascinated me to watch the snowflakes, which resembled swarms of large white bees.

I began to dread the crow's visits, however, the news of my son always discouraging—he was caught scoring heroin and the police had broken his nose; he was contemplating injecting bleach into his arm, so despondent was he; he had checked himself into detox units, rehab programs, hospital psych wards; he was cohabiting with a Mormon bishop, a blond meth freak, a black cat who subsequently died in an alley. I had to cover my ears.

5

There came the day, as I knew it would, when I neglected to tuck the shower curtain inside the bathtub while taking my shower. Hans had gone for the afternoon—god knows where he went for hours at a time (I used to speculate that he had a woman stashed somewhere, a person who tended to his physical needs and complimented him on his taste in reading, his formidable intellect and his sense of humor)—and when I had finished with my ablutions, I heard the angry pounding on the apartment door. Wearing only a towel, I peered though the little eye-hole and perceived a tiny, misshapen woman with a large nose looking back at me.

You have some nerve, she said when I opened the door. My entire apartment is flooded, thanks to you. She was not as tiny as I'd thought, nor as misshapen. She was actually quite attractive in a cheerleader-ish way—a certain type of big girl with crisp incisors renowned for a lack of irony. Permit me to help you clean up the mess, I said. Which is how I came to know Rita and her various boyfriends, one of whom was perched on top of a ladder reading a book on that first visit where, for the rest of this tale, we will leave him.

Rita was a hairdresser with her own business which had been recently revamped by a TV personality that went around revamping hairdresser salons. She was immensely grateful to this personage, claiming that her sales went up exponentially and her employees were far more respectful than before. All this was divulged after I'd done a fair job of sopping up the small lake in Rita's bedroom with two bath towels. When I'd wrung the last of my shower effluent from the towel into a large bucket, Rita was frowning over me. Your hair needs attention, she said.

This is how I happened to become a regular patron of Rita's Hair Salon. I'd been cooped up in Hans' small rooms for so long, I'd forgotten the sheer gleam of the outside world—its rivets and whorls, its dizzying frontal assault when, on my first time out, the snow-bees attacked me. Bigger and bigger they grew until they transformed to giant chickens in front of my eyes, squawking and revving up their wings like jet engines, but silent (paradoxically) perfectly silent, so that the squawks and the revving were only in imagination (nevertheless loud).

And this is a curiosity—how the mind creates its own disturbances and how there is almost a kind of synesthesia involved when it comes to the workings of the imagination, a kind of leakage among compartments. Indeed, in imagination everything connects and overlaps—a disturbing vision is capable of hurting the ear and vice versa, and what was past returns uncannily to infect our present moments. Not only memories but stories, even the stories we held most dear as children and the thought of who we were as children reading those stories, or listening to them, our mothers' warm breath on our necks . . .

Which is why I tried to banish all thoughts of my son.

Thankfully, Rita's salon did not entail much of a trek. It was a pleasant enough place with purple walls and elderly women sitting under hair-driers with pink curlers and Rita running around snapping her precision scissors which she ultimately employed on my own coiff, cutting, shaping and spraying to such an extent that I did not recognize the severe and helmeted visage—like a Roman foot soldier!—that looked back at me from her mirror.

An old woman to whom Rita applied her energetic ministrations, from I believe Finland or Lapland, engaged me in conversation; she talked about her children and her abilities as a fortune teller, a little diminished, she admitted, with her great age. Her children and her children's children and even their children were getting on, she said, and the whole business made her feel very ancient which in fact she was, displaying the ropey veins on her old hands with pride. Fabulous, no? she said. I am lucky to have made it so far as the world is endlessly— here she searched for the right word, then shook her head. The world is endlessly, she repeated, then laughed. Rita was teasing her hair into two towers, then situating tiny plastic windows in each. I like to do my part, said the old woman.

Then she took my hand in both of hers and read my palm. Ah but you, she said. You have just been away on a, shall we say, sojourn during which you completed a great deal of work. It is difficult, almost impossible, to judge this work—I'm not sure why. Then you wandered, looking for that which no longer exists. Then you happened upon a friend, not noted for his warmth and kindness, who took you in. Listen to the crow, she said. Follow the snow bees. Your son awaits you. At this the old woman began to weep so profusely that Rita gently escorted her to the restroom and I made my departure.

6

"The Snow Queen" written by an unattractive, socially inept Dane, said Hans, is a sort of coming-of-age story. There are two children, a boy and a girl, who through a twist of fate become separated. The twist of fate is the Snow Queen herself, an enigmatic personage, beautiful and dangerous—"slender and dazzling"—who entrances the boy, invites him to ride on her sled, wraps him in her fur—"creep into my fur," she entreats seductively, and takes him to her ice palace. We know she is dangerous because on the way to the ice palace, the Snow Queen says "And now you will have no more kisses [...] or else I shall kiss you to death!"

But the best part of the story, said Hans, is that before any of the above occurred, the devils dropped a special mirror which smashed into millions of pieces and became lodged in peoples' eyes and hearts, causing distorted views of the world. For some reason, don't ask me why, I love the idea of that mirror. You love contradictions, I pointed out, and calamities. No, said Hans, I love the idea of lost souls.

The story is a ludicrously obvious tale of sexual seduction, piped up the iris. The beautiful queen, the "fur" that "envelopes" the boy, the sleigh ride to "another land," even the palace with its postlapsarian, postcoital chill. . . . Who among us wants to surrender his penchant for enchantment?

We are all lost souls, Hans went on mournfully, and then he went mournfully to his theremin to play a version of "Over the Rainbow" which sounded like a duck quacking. But I was still thinking about the Snow Queen, who had always reminded me of my mother, who also was given to furs and a cold house and, for years in my young life, inhabited a place of mystery. And this made me think of my son, which I did not want to do, so I changed the course of my thinking and instead thought of the power of the imagination. . . .

So though we cannot exactly envision the matter of "beyond our wildest dreams" (I reflected) since it has not yet been revealed, we can nonetheless attach to this imaginary empty place an ecstatic feeling, it can occupy all our thoughts and direct our smallest actions.

As if reading my mind, a chorus of violets seemed about to chant, *Obsessive Compulsive Disorder* a few times until interrupted by a single rose who seemed about to discourse on that personality disorder, claiming that Gerda demonstrated all the signs of OCD in her persistent quest, her inability to banish little Kay (who was no longer little) from her mind. In a way, the roses seemed about to say, Gerda was obsessed with the irrecoverable past, with childhood in all its one-dimensionality. One could say, the roses seemed about to continue, that she was unable to deal with the complexities of adulthood, especially her own impending adulthood.

Just then the crow appeared at the window, surrounded by its customary band of snow bees, looking a little worn out, as if it had been through an even fiercer blizzard than usual. You are both wrong, said the crow, the SQ is a Gothic story, if you will, wherein a girl has an adventure—becomes, for the moment, the agent of her fate—and in the end discovers the prize wasn't worth it. Ha, added the crow cynically, as if this were the case with pursuits of any kind.

Or, said the cat, who for the first time in our acquaintance seemed to have an opinion, it is the story of incest. That story reminds me of the film *Psycho* only it has a different outcome. The boy escapes the suffocating clutches of the girl and the grandmother and returns to this vale of tears, inevitably resigned. The Freudian drama to a T.

Lost souls! exclaimed Hans. After which we all fell silent.

7

It wasn't until much later that I realized that Hans' love of lost souls might have explained his kindness to me.

I was on my way to Rita's Hair Salon in an even worse blizzard than

162

usual. I could not see one foot in front of me as I walked; I proceeded, therefore, in blind faith, hoping not to fall into an open manhole or stumble in front of a truck. The wind howled and buffeted my head and finally tore my umbrella from my hands and tossed it god-knows-where. I was quite cold and I was enacting that trick where you allow the cold into your body in order to nullify it.

In desperation, I slipped into the premises of an antiquities dealer called Fiske. This was a small, sad establishment that reeked of bygone dust and spiderwebs. Fiske himself emerged from a back room with a fistful of white bread crusts in one hand, wearing a slight smile. How can I help you? he inquired politely. I explained that I was just taking temporary shelter, but I'd be happy to browse.

Indeed, Fiske's Antiquities was a browser's paradise and included stuffed owls and worthogs, troops of books with battered spines, an array of boxes—little ceramic boxes, cloisonné boxes, ivory boxes— perfume bottles with semiprecious jewels dotting their circumferences, a collection of ink pens, and 19th century costumes, notably a chimney sweep costume worn by a manikin with no eyes.

Idly peering into a wooden box decorated with the burnt wood tool of mid 20th century—its lid contained an image of a buck-toothed beaver with the word TOOTHPICKS clumsily embossed—I experienced a jolt of *déjà vu* so severe that I had to grab Fiske by the forearm in order to steady myself.

Even when I'd settled into the wingback chair that Fiske was kind enough to provide, I still could not shake the *déjà vu*. There was an odd familiarity to everything in the shop—the boxes, the pens, the costume and especially the books. I took in their battered spines absent- mindedly as I sat, running my eyes over the titles of books I had never heard of. Even so, they were familiar to me in the way that a story is familiar when you enter it *in medias res* and cannot shake the feeling that you've read it before. . . .

It was hardly a surprise, therefore, when I spotted a copy of H. C. Anderson's fairy tales, illustrated with the tortuous images of Kay Neilsen. It was such a volume from which my mother read "The Snow Queen," a story that terrified me as much as the perfume of my mother.

In the penultimate scene (I recalled), the Snow Queen tells little Kay that if he can spell the word ETERNITY out of icicles she will give him his freedom. This Kay failed to do. Instead, Gerda appeared and melted his heart with the heat of her love.

Fiske said, I can give you a good deal on that book. But I didn't know if I wanted to own it. I'd been away for a long time and I'd accomplished a great deal of work—only the residuals remained and at this point they no longer made sense to me. The memory of them, even now, locked in a suitcase, brought to mind a row of walls with vague, poorly executed scrawls.

Whereas the memory of my son brought to mind the sea . . .

When last seen, he was living in a black Camry, terribly thin, begging for food by sticking his hand out of the window. His face, reported the crow, had hardened into a contemptuous mask, and when passersby declined to drop a dollar into his outstretched palm, he spit at them. These depressing reports nullified all memories of the sea—though my son persisted at the back my mind, despite my best efforts to banish him.

Oh beauty, oh sadness! I thought, apropos of nothing. Though perhaps it was the beautiful boy making sandcastles that flashed before my eyes. His knees scraped up.

It was still snowing. Possibly it would always snow. It is hard to know what to do under any circumstances, much less those circumstances which require us to fight against the prevailing weather. His knees were scraped because he had fallen from his bicycle.

I'd dabbed on peroxide and plastered a few bandaids. The world was shining and perfect, the sea left a moustache of white foam on the shore. In a while we'd go home, make sandwiches, tell stories. Did I read him the story of the Snow Queen? I think not. It would have frightened him. Although my mother who looked uncannily like the Snow Queen read the story to me.

In those days I would have done anything to protect my son.

If I were to encounter him now—in an alley, say, covered with snow—I would not be able to melt his heart. My love, unlike Gerda's, has gone cold. It appears that we are doomed to go our separate ways, to continue in the darkness of our own making, half-blind, and no longer who we once were.

That's the way most stories end, I mused sadly. Not with roses blooming, not with the onset of summer, not hand-in-hand.

In moments, I would pay Fiske the required amount, tuck the book inside my jacket and head into the fray.

IMMINENCE

Red-shouldered hawk sits on a wire waiting for the doves which he will kill. We sit in the car watching the hawk await its prey. Red-shouldered hawk, very stationary, very beautiful, very noble, with a bold slice of orangey red on each shoulder. We light cigarettes and observe. We observe the spaces in the sky which are empty. We observe the smoke filling the car's interior like an image (such as the hawk) fills the caverns of our imaginations. With our usual composure, we observe the ruthlessness of nature: one creature about to swoop upon another. Red-shouldered hawk snaps his head to the left. In the distance, the tender clamors of doves about to descend. Is all life so misguided? we wonder. We light fresh cigarettes. The real show is about to begin.

ACKNOWLEDGMENTS:

The author wishes to thank the following publications in which some of these stories have appeared:

Crowd, Cutthroat, Four Way Review, Interim, New World Writing, Ocean City Review, Ploughshares, Prompt Press, Slant, Sonora Review, Story Quarterly, and *TriQuarterly.*

"Pete, Waste Lab Technician," appears in *Winesberg, Indiana,* (Indiana University Press, 2015).

"10 Birds" appears in *Wreckage of Reason: XXperimental Prose by Contemporary Women Authors,* ed. Nava Renek, (Spuytin Duyvil, 2008).

"The Snow Queen" appears in *My Mother She Killed Me, My Father He Ate Me,* ed. Kate Bernheimer, (Penguin Books, 2010).

I am immensely grateful to friends and esteemed artists/writers who have inspired me along the way, especially The Warren Wilson MFA Program for Writers which has given me a spectacular family. A special thanks to Martha Rhodes, my brilliant editor, to Ryan Murphy who designs gorgeous books, and to all the rest of you up there in the Tribeca loft, slaving away in the name of literature. To Steve Romaniello and Beth Alvarado who have many times loaned me their generous, insightful ears, and offered encouragement. And to Rachel, my heart, whose presence is everywhere in these pages.

Karen Brennan is the author of six books of varying genres, including poetry collections *Here on Earth* (1989), *The Real Enough World* (2006), and *little dark* (2014); AWP Award–winning short fiction *Wild Desire* (1990); story collection *The Garden in Which I Walk* (2005); and a memoir, *Being with Rachel* (2001). Brennan is a recipient of a National Endowment for the Arts fellowship in fiction, and her fiction, poetry, and nonfiction have appeared in anthologies from Graywolf, Norton, Penguin, Spuytin Duyvil, University of Georgia, and University of Michigan, among others. She is professor emerita at the University of Utah and teaches in the MFA Program for Writers at Warren Wilson College. Her website is karenbrennan.org.

Publication of this book was made possible by grants and donations. We are also grateful to those individuals who participated in our 2015 Build a Book Program. They are:

Jan Bender-Zanoni, Betsy Bonner, Deirdre Brill, Carla & Stephen Carlson, Liza Charlesworth, Catherine Degraw & Michael Connor, Greg Egan, Martha Webster & Robert Fuentes, Anthony Guetti, Hermann Hesse, Deming Holleran, Joy Jones, Katie Childs & Josh Kalscheur, Michelle King, David Lee, Howard Levy, Jillian Lewis, Juliana Lewis, Owen Lewis, Alice St. Claire Long & David Long, Catherine McArthur, Nathan McClain, Carolyn Murdoch, Tracey Orick, Kathleen Ossip, Eileen Pollack, Barbara Preminger, Vinode Ramgopal, Roni Schotter, Soraya Shalforoosh, Marjorie & Lew Tesser, David Tze, Abby Wender, and Leah Nanako Winkler.